BONE POINT

Bone Point

by

Bette Golden Lamb
&
J. J. Lamb

TWO BLACK SHEEP PRODUCTIONS
NOVATO, CALIFORNIA

i

Books By
Bette Golden Lamb & J. J. Lamb

Books in the Gina Mazzio RN Medical Thriller Series:
Bone Dry
Sin & Bone
Bone Pit
Bone of Contention
Bone Dust
Bone Crack
Bone Slice

Other novels by Bette Golden Lamb & J. J. Lamb
Sisters in Silence
Heir Today...
The Killing Vote

By Bette Golden Lamb
The Organ Harvesters
The Organ Harvesters-Book II
The Russian Girl

By J. J. Lamb
Books in the Zachariah Tobias Rolfe III Series
A Nickel Jackpot
The Chinese Straight
Losers Take All
No Pat Hands

Bone Point

Cover design:
Sue Trowbridge
www.Interbridge.com

www.twoblacksheep.us

Dedication

To all U. S. military veterans - from every war,
conflict, and peacetime involvement - you deserve the
best possible treatment for your service, not as a reward
or entitlement, but as a commitment from your country
and fellow citizens.

Acknowledgements

Thomas Kearney, Jr., PharmD, DABAT, FAACT,
Associate Dean, Department of Clinical Pharmacy,
University of California San Francisco; and, of course,
our ever-helpful Critique Group – Gwen Kauffman, Rita
Lakin, Margaret (Peggy) Lucke, and Nicola Trwst. Extra
acknowledgement to Sue Trowbridge, always there to
save our sanity. Add to this the loving encouragement of
our sons, Clifford and Michael.

Prologue

Guy West, Veteran, U.S.M.C.

Blinding lights were digging holes into his brain–they bounced off the walls, off the piece of paper they shoved in front of him.

"Sign here!"

His head buzzed.

Do-it-do-it-do-it.

It was all shutting down. Felt like he was in a hot, sun-filled hole. Here to get fried, get juiced up again. Maybe this time it'll kill him.

He signed the paper. They warned him again that the seizures could damage his brain; he could become apathetic and indifferent. Some smartass somewhere in the room even called it an electric lobotomy.

What's the difference? All that was left inside of him was fear, panic, and memories of a bloody war.

Wanted it all to go away. Wanted to be dead.

The voices wouldn't stop. They were all around him. He was getting creeped out with everyone handling him, touching him one place or another.

Started an IV that he barely felt.

Bunches of leads were smacked onto his body and the pounding of his heart was way too loud with an electronic beep … beep … beep … beep.

Someone with rough hands tried to whisper words to him and then strapped something on his head.

Everyone was talking around him, talking to each other.

1

Blood pressure cuff was tight as it automatically inflated; someone jammed a mask onto his face. Cold air escaped and blew up into his eyes; something was shoved into his hands.

His mind wouldn't stop jumping.

He hated this. Hated his life.

His stomach gave off a loud growl. Someone laughed.

Nothing in his mouth since last night. He was beginning to feel nauseous. He wanted to barf.

He thought of his vets group. There his stomach would growl, too. The men's voices would turn into drill bits boring deep holes in his head.

All he really had was his vets group. They met once a week and after that he would feel grounded for a day, but then his mind would be gone again.

He could still hear Vinnie's voice echoing in his head: "You're gonna make it, man." Vinnie Mazzio, his last brother from the war.

Vinnie, you're my only friend.

In his circle of vets … he couldn't stand to look them in the eye anymore … even started to hate Vinnie. He didn't want to be close to anyone… not after he nearly choked Gigi to death … she took their little boy and left.

Please come back … please come back … please come back.

But she was gone.

Guy imagined Vinnie was there looking at him. "Guy, you gotta stop drinking with that shitload of meds you're taking. It's gonna kill you."

"We're going to put you to sleep now."

Something was jammed between his teeth.

Everything was sharp again.

He sat up, ripped the IV from his arm and shouted, "No! No more! Get me out here!"

* * *

Thor said, "Did ya give them the extra dope?"

2

"Do I look stupid? How the hell we going to do anything with any of those maniacs awake and screaming?"

"Do ya look stupid?" Thor wouldn't let it go. His twang was edgy, became a dry, silent laugh. "Shit, yeah, man. Ya look about as dumb as a post."

"Maaayybe, but I'm not an inbred, like you. Isn't that what they do in Kentucky? Fuck their sisters?"

Delores Smiley, the Nursing Supervisor, walked up to the two of them, shook her head and pointed a finger, first at one, then the other. "You have a job to do. Stop fussing." She walked out the door.

Thor wondered why these VA hospitals never hired any good-lookin' bitches. And this one sorry-ass excuse for a woman was in their face way too often.

He and Eddie moved ahead into one of the Tunnel rooms where three patients had been brought down earlier.

They were all out cold.

These three were supposed to be the sickest bunch in the nut box screaming in their sleep, punching at the air around them, trying to stop something in their heads from killin' them. Even with the mega hits of downers they got each night, which could probably stop an elephant, they were still restless and miserable.

Thor flashed on the beds with his Maglite, but there was nothing in the way of movement. The extra meds these guys were given had really zonked them out.

"C'mon, dickhead," Thor said to Eddie.

They moved straight to one of the gurneys. The name card on the chart at his foot said: Guy West, Corporal, USMC.

They each took a position.

"Hand over the damn pillow," Thor said.

"Ya better stop ordering me around," Eddie said. After a glare, he grabbed a pillow from the bedside chair, covered the face of the vet, who was lying flat on his back.

There was hardly a struggle as they both pressed down.

3

Soon, the corporal was no longer out cold, like the other two in the room. He was plain old dead.

"Thank ya for your service, buddy."

Chapter 1

San Francisco, Sunday, 9 pm

It was still a couple of hours before bedtime for a lot of people. Most were watching TV, hanging out, playing cards, and even making love.

Not Gina and Harry.

At 9 p.m. they were snuggled down in their bed with their cat Tuva burrowed between them. The little gray tabby had planted herself smack in the middle, making it impossible for them to cuddle up against each other.

Gina was used to the cat vying for their attention and they both loved the little rescue animal. She'd been theirs for about four years now and it was only in the last year she'd stopped sleeping under the bed. She finally trusted them.

Someone must have really hurt their little girl.

They were both scratching her neck and trying to read at the same time. She was purring like a motorboat at high throttle.

Gina was having trouble concentrating. Although she loved being pregnant and was still amazed it had happened, reading about pre-natal care wasn't her thing.

An RN shouldn't have to read this basic common sense kind of stuff the OB/Gyn doc gave us.

And not just one RN. Harry's an RN too.

Her mind drifted and the words blurred in front of her.

That night in a Bronx ER, so many years ago, when she'd almost bled out, should have seemed like another lifetime. But the memory of her drunken ex-husband raping her with a Coke bottle never went away. The docs told her she was lucky to be alive and to forget about having children.

She tried to shove aside the memory, but once her mind drifted there, it was almost impossible to ignore.

She'd packed her bags and fled to San Francisco □a knee-jerk reaction. She couldn't bear to look at anyone, or have others look at her, even after they threw Dominick in jail.

She looked at Harry now, felt his body near her.

After they'd met, she tried so hard to back away, but she'd come to need him. Every breath he took nourished her soul.

"That's enough!"

She flung the pamphlet across the room, watched it bounce off the wall. As it hit the floor, Harry's similar pamphlet went flying, landing right on top of hers as though they'd carefully stacked them.

Gina lay back, stared up at the ceiling. Soon Harry's hand was resting on her baby bump.

"She's going to be beautiful like you."

"I don't think so." She placed a hand on top of his. "He's going to look just like his dad with your beautiful blue eyes."

"Man, are we lucky." They said it together and Gina laughed.

She nudged Tuva to the foot of the bed and they were in each other's arms.

The phone rang.

"Let it go to the answering machine," he whispered in her ear.

"Mmmm, yes."

It finally stopped ringing, but in a couple of breaths it started all over again.

Gina reached out and grabbed it. "Hello?"

"It's me."

Her best friend's voice. She swung her legs around and sat up.

"Helen, what's wrong?"

Harry lifted up, too, his face lined with worry.

Helen began to cry.

6

"What is it? Tell me!"

"Vinnie's gone."

* * *

Gina and Harry were dressed and out the door in minutes. Gina floored the Fiat's accelerator. She hoped the fussy little car wouldn't break down, or worse, she'd get a speeding ticket.

"This is not like Vinnie," Harry said. "Your brother's not some irresponsible kid. Something serious has happened."

"I've noticed he's been a little down lately, but he goes through phases of depression. PTSD still seems to rule his life most of time." Gina slammed on the brakes. She'd almost gone through a red light. "It's been four years since Vinnie returned from Afghanistan. Will it never end?"

"He's done well, made good progress since he came to San Francisco and joined that support group." Harry put his arm around her shoulder. "You know, doll, it never really goes away. There's always a trigger out there, waiting to set him off. Then everything he went through beats him up all over again. And again. And again."

As they circled around the block, hunting for a parking space, Gina recalled how she'd introduced Helen to Vinnie after he started working as a nurse tech with her at Ridgewood Hospital. The two hit it off immediately.

Gina was close to tears when a spot finally opened up. She slipped the little car into the space in one swoop. As soon as she turned off the ignition, they were out of the car and running.

Helen must have been looking for them from her window because she was standing at the open apartment door. Waiting.

Gina and Helen reached out for each other, both hanging on and hugging as tight as they could. When they separated, Harry kissed Helen on the cheek.

"What happened?" Gina asked.

The three of them moved to the living room and sat.

"How could he leave like that?" Helen said, her face drained of blood.

7

"What happened?" Gina asked again.

"The only explanation he gave was in this note." She held it up. "He handed it to me."

"When was that?" Harry asked

"He just walked out ... about an hour ago."

Helen was up and pacing back and forth. Her movements were erratic, as though someone had spiked her with a live electric wire. "I mean, I should have called the police, done something. But what did I do? Sat with my hands folded. Nothing." After a few moments she finally quieted down, sat, and tossed the note to Gina. "See what you think."

Harry looked over Gina's shoulder as she read.

Dearest Helen,

Please forgive me, but I have to go to where Guy died. I must know what happened to him. I'll call soon.

I love you.

Vinnie

Harry said, "Guy? That must be Guy West. He and Vinnie were in the same unit in Afghanistan. They were the only two who survived an IED. They really bonded."

"Wait a minute," Helen said. "How do you know Guy?"

"Remember Pablo, who runs the support group? He's a friend of Harry's," Gina said. "That's how Vinnie was able to get in so quickly. There's a two-year wait for that particular group; they have the best treatment stats in the Bay Area for PTSD."

"Last week Pablo told Vinnie that Guy died." Helen clutched a soaked tissue. "It really hit your brother hard, Gina. He's been depressed ever since. I could barely get him to eat and he spends half the night pacing back and forth through the house."

"I knew it! I knew there was something wrong," Gina said. "Why didn't you tell us about this sooner?"

Helen stared at them. "You two have been so happy for the past three months ... I didn't want to do anything to burst your bubble."

"But we'd do anything for Vinnie, anything for you," Harry said. "You know that."

"You're our best friend, Helen. We're always here for you." Gina squeezed Helen's arm. "Do you have any idea where he could be?"

"Not really," Helen said. "He's pretty tight-lipped about those meetings and what goes on."

"I've tried, too," Gina said. "He clams up the minute I bring it up. Has he said anything to you, Harry?"

"No. I try to respect his privacy. The man's been through hell. Afghanistan lives in a big part of his brain and will probably be there forever. I don't probe. But he knows I'm there if he needs me."

They all dropped into silence, lost in their own thoughts.

Gina was the first to speak. "Come stay with us," she said, squeezing her friend's hand.

"No. I can't do that. I have to be here when he comes back."

"He'll know where you are," Harry said.

Helen sat up straight. "No. I want to be *here*." All at once she burst into tears. "I *have* to be here."

Chapter 2

Sunday Night, Coast Road

Vinnie's thighs hugged his motorcycle as he rode the twisting road through the California coastal hills. The windswept rain was exhilarating and he was glad to be alone with his thoughts, away from San Francisco.

The road guided him through a deserted part of the Sonoma coast. Homes were scarce and he saw only a few of them when his headlights bounced off their sides. He knew the forest grew right up to the edge of the jagged cliffs and he could still make out large swatches of wooded land that no one had yet tamed.

It felt pristine … pure.

It took many miles before his chest relaxed and he could finally breathe deeply. He took in large gulps of the wind until his head was light and he felt high and free.

It was pitch black when he found a spot to camp. He laid out his gear on the ground, high up on a cliff that probably overlooked the ocean. The air was sweet and he felt safe.

The plan had been to lie in his sleeping bag, next to his bike, and stare up at the stars peeking through the tops of the swaying trees. But there would be no stars tonight. Still, he was content. The rain was much softer under the trees and the sounds and smell of wet earth was comforting.

He'd chosen his bivouac well.

He wasn't like his sister Gina, who shied away from wide open spaces, felt safer with people hanging around, at least in small numbers.

Gina was tough, but his big sister was also an optimist.

She thought people would help her if she needed it, just the way *she* wanted to help them. She'd be the first to tell you that was

11

the reason she became a nurse. His fiancée, Helen, felt the same way.

No surprise why they're such good friends.

But it wasn't the same for him. He wasn't like his fiancée and his sister. Although he liked to care for his patients and was happy being a patient tech at Ridgewood Hospital, he knew most people didn't give a rat's ass about anything but themselves.

Gina had grown soft since she left the Bronx, moved to California. Even more so since she married Harry. All the horrors of her ex had taken a long step back now that he was dead and she rarely talked about Dominick anymore. Remembering her pregnancy, he smiled at the thought of becoming an uncle.

The rain stopped and the clouds parted, revealing an exquisite night sky. Even with only a crescent moon, light filled the sky. He could see everything all around him. He was surrounded by tall pines that felt like guardians. He couldn't sense anyone nearby.

He thought about his buddy, Guy. He'd been close to the man since they'd met in Afghanistan. It hurt to think he was gone.

Why had he voluntarily signed up for a closed psych unit in one of the oldest VA facilities in California? Vinnie had known there was something troubling him, but no matter how hard he tried, Guy wouldn't open up to him or the group.

Now he was dead.

Vinnie wanted to cry. At least he knew his friend wasn't suffering anymore. The war had worn him down. Worn down every person who was there.

He looked again at a fragment of sky when the swaying pines opened. Soon he felt peaceful and drifted off to sleep.

* * *

BOOM!

His eyes snapped open. He'd heard an explosion.

His whole body was instantly covered in sweat. His insides churned. He gagged and swallowed hard against the sudden burning bile searing his throat. With deep breaths he slowly reached behind him and with a shaking hand pulled his combat knife from its scabbard. Adrenalin surged through his veins; his head pounded.

BOOM!

Sound was blasting all around him.

They were out there, waiting to kill him.

"Kill them!" Kill the murdering bastards who had slaughtered his buddies. They were stalking him now.

He closed his eyes, fought to silence the outbursts erupting in his head. But the visions were waiting for him. Visions of death everywhere, his buddy's head exploding like a ripe melon. Blood and brains splattering everywhere.

He hugged himself to keep from splintering into pieces, to feel that he was still alive.

A vision of the soldier's head appeared, exploding over and over.

"No. No. No!"

He was choking, couldn't breathe. He tried to scream, but his throat was squeezed shut.

Been hit ... dying.

His eyes were glued shut. They wouldn't open.

Could hear them ... close ... somewhere on his left. How many were there?

Wrong ... something was wrong.

He was confused ... everything smelled wrong. There was a whiff of an ocean. Why could he hear foliage shuffling in a desolate landscape?

Shaking, he turned slowly onto his stomach, his knife at the ready.

He forced his eyes open.

A doe and its fawn were searching for shoots of grass between a carpet of pine needles and scattered twigs. She turned her soft brown doe eyes to stare at him, then went back to butting her nose at the ground.

13

With sweaty, trembling hands he slid the knife back into its sheath.

He watched the deer until they moved deeper into the woods.

Chapter 3

Monday Morning

Gina and Harry snatched an outside table at the HA-HA Cafe. She loved the name of the funky place, and they also served the best breakfasts in San Francisco's Sunset District. Today, Gina only had a latte in front of her. She sipped it while Harry finished his scrambled eggs.

He looked up at her, his face wrinkled with worry. "Gina, you have to eat. Think of the baby. Please let me order something for you."

"How can I eat when my brother has gone missing?"

"If you're going to carry this pregnancy to term, you *have* to think of yourself … you could end up in serious trouble"

"I'm trying, Harry."

"It was difficult enough when you were twelve weeks pregnant and had to have your cervix stitched." Harry tipped her chin to look into her eyes. "I know how hard that was for you. But this whole thing with Vinnie is so much harder than that procedure … I mean, emotionally this is out of the ballpark. You *have t*o take care of yourself. Let me take care of you."

"I know. I know. But I can't help being worried."

He reached for her hand, kissed her open palm. "There are good reasons they wanted you to stop working. And you know every one of them." He held onto her hand and leaned back into his chair. "Emotional stress is part of it. *And,* I still cringe when you pick up that purse of yours."

"They said no more than ten pounds. It only weighs six."

He laughed. "I know you hate to hear this, doll, but you have to take it easy. I mean, it's so hard to leave you for an out-of-town assignment in the midst of all of this—"

"No, no, Harry. You only gave TravelNurse, Inc. a three-day commitment. I'll be fine." Gina sipped her drink again. "Don't mess up taking these short-term gigs or you won't get them anymore. And I know you won't be happy with a full-time job at Ridgewood."

She looked away, wanted to cry but wouldn't let herself. "I hate not working. I love my job ... and having to lie around like a potted plant ... well, it's horrible. I feel useless."

"But think how lucky we are that you even *got* pregnant."

"Well, shoot! The kid might as well start holding up her end of things right now." She laughed. "Oops, I said *her*."

Harry laughed. "That's what we get for refusing to know the sex of the heir to the Mazzio-Lucke fortunes. We'll just keep on guessing."

Gina couldn't help but smile.

Harry looked at his watch. "Pablo should be here any moment."

"The two of you met in nursing school, right?"

"Yup. When we graduated, I chose to work mostly in intensive care. Pablo began to specialize in psychological trauma after his brother died in Iraq. He decided to become a counselor. Hey, speaking of the devil, there he is."

"Where?"

Harry pointed. "That's him over there. He's the tall, dark-skinned, handsome dude. He makes me feel puny."

"He *is* gorgeous." She squeezed his hand. "But you've got muscles in all the right places."

He leaned over and kissed her cheek.

Harry stood and pulled out a chair as Pablo walked up to them. They shook hands and did a bro bump. "Hi, man. Great to see you. Thanks for coming."

Pablo reached out a hand to Gina. "Pablo Chavez. Nice to meet Vinnie's sister. At our meetings, he does nothing but brag about you." He turned back to Harry. "You, too, man. He's lucky

16

to have the both of you. And, of course, his fantastic fiancée, Helen."

"Sit down. Order something; it's on us," Gina said. "It's the least we can do for your taking the time to see us."

"Already ate. And I can't stay long."

"Vinnie's missing," Harry blurted.

Pablo looked stunned. "Are you kidding me? No way. That man is doing great in the support meetings. I have really high hopes for him."

"It has something to do with Guy West's death." Gina had to slow herself down. She wanted to pound the vet counselor with questions. Instead, she sipped her latte and took a few deep breaths.

"Yeah." The counselor was lost in thought for a moment. "I knew when I told Vinnie it would hit him hard. But Guy has been in trouble for a long time." Pablo reached for a napkin from the holder and started absent-mindedly wiping the table in front of him.

"You know he had me listed as his designated advocate." Pablo's eyes stared off into space. "After his wife and child left him and he refused to have anything to do with his parents, he just kind of floundered."

"I don't know how you deal with so much pain day after day." Harry threw an arm around his shoulder. "Man, I couldn't do it."

"Some days are harder than others. This was very hard. I'm the one Bone Point notified of his death."

"Bone Point?" Gina said.

Pablo nodded. "It's VA psychiatric facility on the coast north of here."

"Did they give you a cause of death?" Harry asked.

"Vinnie asked the same thing when I called to break the news to him. As a matter of fact, they were damn evasive about it." Pablo shifted in his seat. "I never did get a real answer."

Gina leaned forward. "The man was so young ... I mean ..." She tried to hold back but she couldn't. "Well, I know Guy was in the group for PTSD. But did anything unusual happen recently?"

"Those meeting are totally confidential ... just like I told you on the phone, Harry."

"Confidential?" Gina blurted. "The man's dead, for god's sake. We need some answers. You're the only one who can help us. We're trying to find my brother. Don't you get it?"

Harry took her hand and squeezed it. "Come on, doll ... please quiet down."

Pablo studied her with an intense gaze before he spoke. "Yeah, I get it."

"Man, we'd really appreciate anything you can tell us." Harry said. "All we want to do is help Vinnie."

Pablo tapped his fingers on the table for a long moment before he said, "I will share something that won't break the vow I give these vets."

"Please," Harry said.

"Maybe I will have a quick cup of coffee,"

Harry nodded to the waiter, who came over to their table. "What can I get you?"

"I'll have an espresso, please," Pablo said.

The waiter was back in what seemed like an instant. He set the small white cup and saucer in front of Pablo.

"Thanks," Pablo said, taking a sip as though it weren't piping hot. "Guy checked into Bone Point over two weeks ago."

"Tell me about Bone Point?" Gina said.

"It's one of the VA's inpatient psychiatric hospitals."

Harry looked floored. "I thought they shut down that rundown hellhole. It's had a horrible rep." He leaned forward until he was almost in Pablo's face. "How could you let any of your group check in there?"

Pablo's shoulders tightened. "Look, dude, it was the only place that would take him on the spot." He abruptly stood. "You might have noticed getting into an inpatient vet hospital isn't a

18

walk in the park. All of them are way overcrowded. Grabbing a bed without going through a bunch of bullshit is a nightmare. They only let him in because they had beds available."

"All I hear is about the lack of VA beds," Gina said.

"They're closing Bone Point in the next few months so they had the room. I was surprised they were accepting *any* admissions."

"What about outpatient care?" she said. "Wouldn't that be better than Bone Point? It sounds like it should be condemned."

The counselor glared at her, pushed himself up.

"Hey, come on, man, sit down," Harry said.

"You might be a friend, Harry, but that doesn't mean you and Gina get to blame me ... even if we could get him into something on an outpatient basis, it wouldn't have worked for Guy. That dude was suicidal, getting really bat-shit crazy and dangerous. He tried to knife someone at a bar and only got off because the guy was a veteran and refused to press charges. But sooner or later, Guy was going to do something that would land him in jail."

"Sorry. We're just upset about Vinnie." Harry gently tugged at his arm. "Please sit back down."

"Forgive me, Pablo. But you've got to help us. We're so worried," Gina said. "I don't understand. Why would Vinnie do this?"

"As I said before, Vinnie is making great progress," Pablo said, dropping back into the seat. "Damn, why am I even discussing this with you?"

"Please, anything you can do ... we'd be really grateful," Harry said.

"Guy West was like a brother to Vinnie," the counselor said. "They served in the same unit in Afghanistan ... swore to be there for each other ... no matter what."

"I didn't know that," Gina said. "Why didn't he tell me?"

Pablo downed the rest of his coffee. "You've got to understand, Gina. These vets will give outsiders what they think they can stand to hear ... or more to the point, what *they* can take sharing. And remember, first and foremost, they never let each other down."

"But Guy died last week," Harry said. "I don't get it. What is there to gain?"

"I can't answer that for you." The counselor stood again, ready to leave. "Only Vinnie can."

Chapter 4

Monday Morning

Vinnie stared up at the Bone Point VA hospital. It was a gloomy sight, built with yellow brick that was chipped and covered with black mold; tentacles of dried-up ivy still managed to cling to most of the front wall.

A chill crawled down his spine when he looked at the bars on the second, third, and fifth floor windows.

So this is where it all ended for Guy.

Now he understood why the men in the group who had seen the facility called it "a snake pit filled with crazies." To Vinnie, that's how a place like that would look malevolent and creepy, ready to grow fangs and attack.

He sat on the edge of a crumbling fountain and thought about the past night. He'd kept trying to get his head around why his friend had just up and left without a word to him.

Vinnie knew Guy was confused and couldn't put his life together, especially after his wife left him. Guy had confessed to Pablo and the group that he couldn't sleep most nights and in the last month he'd started drinking heavily again. When he was into booze, he lost any control he might have had. All he wanted to do was strike out. Even a baby in a carriage became the enemy.

Neither Vinnie nor the group had been able to help him and that's what they were there for. They'd all let Guy down.

Guy had told Vinnie that everything inside of him was getting out of whack again. His nightmares came every night now, and sometimes it was hard to tell what was reality and what was only in his head. Like a loop it kept repeating itself, over and over.

Vinnie pictured that day in the dirty Humvee in Afghanistan.

21

The four of them had been sweltering inside the vehicle for almost four hours, looking for snipers and IEDs.

The last thing he could remember was the flash and boom of an IED exploding.

Vinnie had only been cut and bloodied, but the explosion had left him in shock. He couldn't remember pulling Guy out of the mess, gunning down attackers, or calling for help. But after the helicopter lift back to the hospital bivouac, others seemed to know what happened.

They had put it together.

People in the unit said over and over that Guy would have died like the other two men without Vinnie. He would have bled out if Vinnie hadn't wrapped a tourniquet around Guy's shredded arm.

Vinnie still couldn't visualize any of it. It was like it had happened to someone else.

But that was then, this was now. Right now he hadn't been able to save Guy.

Vinnie wanted to get on with his life, marry Helen, and just be normal again. But now that the last man from his unit was gone, all he could think about was Afghanistan and his dead buddies.

They were *all* gone now.

The black hole inside of him was growing again.

I should have died with the rest of them.

* * *

Donnie stared out a filthy window on the deserted fifth floor. He ran his hand through his white beard and mumbled, "Poor man."

Soon there was a humming sound vibrating deep in his throat.

"Run! Don't come in here. Run away while you can."

He was safe here in his hideaway on this closed-off floor of the hospital. No one ever came here except that nice woman, Ziggy.

She talked to him softly, brought him fresh clothes to wear. She was his only friend. Well, except the gray shadows. They were soft and quiet. They embraced him, hid him from the dangerous world.

That's where the pain lived.

He looked down at the man who had pulled up on a motorcycle and stepped off right alongside the broken fountain. Leaning closer, Donnie rested his nose against the cold window pane and rubbed his hands together for warmth. A chill coursed up his spine.

He was sad for the man.

He was too high up to see the biker's features, other than the dark, wavy hair when he tore off his helmet; he guessed the rider was probably somewhere in his late twenties, and he looked strong.

People don't come to visit here and patients don't show up in anything other than an ambulance or a car with someone else driving. They act drunk and need a lot of muscle getting them to move at all.

The motorcycle man seemed uncertain about coming inside, but soon he set his helmet on the bike seat and headed for the entrance.

Whoever you are, don't come in here.

"Leave," he whispered.

A humming sound again vibrated in Donnie's throat.

"Go back."

* * *

Vinnie walked through the front entrance. The lobby was shabby, the floor dotted with flakes of paint from the grimy ceiling. A pinned-up sign said "Reception" and had an arrow pointing the way. He headed in that direction but was intercepted by a pair of uniformed security guards, who walked up to him with a slow, easy stride of confidence. They were both big men, the type you would expect to find outside a nightclub, with go-don't-go authority.

"Can we help you?" one of them said, his face flushing as he spit out the words.

"Yeah, man. I need to be admitted."

* * *

The guards ushered Vinnie into an office, left him there, and went back outside. Vinnie noticed there were three desks in the room but there were no papers or any other signs that anyone was using two of them. The woman at the third desk looked up at him and moved the clutter of file folders in front of her off to the side. Her name was displayed on a plaque sitting on the edge of her desk:

Ziggy Jones
Administrative Assistant

She had a kind face, with deep lines etched in her dark skin and she seemed very nervous.

The security guys were standing at a window, looking in. They seemed to be waiting for further orders.

"It's okay," Ziggy Jones said to the men, waving one hand at the window. "You can leave now."

The men gave Vinnie another once-over and moved away.

The woman didn't introduce herself, but she wore a name tag that matched the desk plaque information. She asked him for his personal information; her long red nails clicked his answers rapidly on the computer keyboard. Soon a large lineup of forms was spit out of the printer. She placed them in front of her and read them.

"Vincent Mazzio. Is that a good Italian name?" she said softly without humor.

"It's the one I was born with."

"You don't sound like you're from around here," she said, lifting the papers from the machine.

He shook his head. "New York."

"How long have you been in California?"

"A few years."

24

"I see you're already in an outpatient recovery program." She looked at him for a few moments. He could feel her assessing him. "Sir, we don't have many vets walk through our doors volunteering to be hospitalized. We're kind of off the beaten path. What made you come to us?"

"I was camping not far from here when I started freaking out, thought about jumping off a cliff. VA locators directed me here."

"Well, killing yourself is one thing … what about killing others? Do you want to hurt people? Or anyone in particular?" She threw the questions at him rapid fire.

"I don't know what I'm capable of." He looked away. "I feel sick and afraid. I need help."

"If you're absolutely sure you want to be admitted, please sign the papers at each red X." She pushed the stack to his side of the desk.

He signed without reading them and handed the pile back to her. She witnessed his signature.

She eyed where he'd filled in the blanks. "You've given no next of kin."

"That's right."

"We have to have someone we can call."

Vinnie shook his head. "Well, there's no one."

Her eyes were still questioning as she picked up the phone and dialed a number.

* * *

Vinnie was escorted by two hulking orderlies, who wore grubby white scrubs. When they stepped onto the elevator, each of them took hold of an arm.

"Now you're not going to give us any trouble, are you?" The man had a southern twang and looked like he'd cut his hair himself … with dull shears. He inserted and turned a key, then pressed number two on the button board. "My name is Eddie Forrest. And just because my name is Eddie don't mean I'm your friend. Got it?"

Vinnie nodded and glanced at the other man, who looked angry. "What's *your* name?"

"What's the matter with you?" He poked a finger into Vinnie's ribs, and then fixed his name tag so it was right side up. "Can't you read?"

"Now I can."

Thornly Mason gave him the eye. It said that messing with him would be a bad mistake.

"You can call me Thornly." Then he snickered. "You can, but it won't get anything but the wrong kind of attention. My name is Thor. You know, like the Norse god. Hear me?"

"I get it."

"It's Thor or nothing." He leaned in closer to Vinnie. "Make sure that's really clear in your head, nut boy."

"I said, I got it."

Thor's nostrils flared. His lips were drawn into a straight line. It took moments before his face finally relaxed.

When they reached the second floor, the elevator door eased open and Eddie withdrew the key. Both men tugged at Vinnie's arms and pulled him into the corridor.

Vinnie looked down the hallway. There were three gurneys up next to the walls. The black mats on them were all taped where the leather must have split open. As they walked down the hall, he couldn't help but notice the majority of the floor's black and white ceramic tiles were chipped. Many had been taken out and the bare cement was exposed.

They came to a halt at an open doorway. The first thing Vinnie saw in the room was bars on the outer double windows. Two men were slumped in chairs next to their beds. Another pair of empty beds had patient gowns spread out in the middle of them.

The smell in the room almost made him faint. It was a ripe combination of mold, piss, and shit.

What the hell am I doing here?

Chapter 5

Tuesday Morning

Gina sprawled on the living room sofa with Tuva. The tabby curled up next to her while she read a new novel called *Snow Angel*. It was awkward scratching the cat's neck and turning the pages at the same time, but it was comforting to have Tuva there.

The phone rang. She glanced at the call window   Pablo Chavez.

"Gina?"

"Pablo! Have you heard from Vinnie?"

"I thought you would want know that he's checked himself into Bone Point."

Gina's heart was racing. "Did he call you?"

"No, but I have a few connections here and there."

"You're absolutely certain?"

There was a long silence.

"Pablo, it's not that I don't trust you, but I just have to know for sure."

"It's solid info."

* * *

Gina stared at her phone for a long time after she hung up. Tuva followed her as she began pacing back and forth.

She plopped back down on the sofa and called Harry.

"What are you doing, Ms. Lucke? That is, besides going crazy hanging around the house?"

"House arrest has been known to do that ... I mean drive people crazy. So I've been absorbing one book after another, trying not to think about my baby brother."

"I can't stop thinking about Vinnie either."

"Pablo called, told me Vinnie checked himself into that damn Bone Point."

"Well, at least we know where he is."

"Isn't there some way we can pull him out of that horrible place?" She looked into Tuva's worried green eyes. The cat knew something was wrong. "It's the not knowing what's happening to him that's driving me nuts."

"I understand, but since he voluntarily signed himself in, he's the only one who can do anything about it. There's nothing we can do."

"Helen's coming over later. I guess the two of us will cry our eyes out together."

"I'm glad she'll be with you."

"I'm worried about her. I know Helen. She probably hasn't put anything into her mouth since he left. I'm going to cook up some spaghetti with my favorite Bolognese sauce. I know she loves that. I swear if she doesn't eat I'll force feed her."

"You'll be good for each other, cheer you both up."

Hearing Harry's voice drew her attention to their silver framed wedding pictures perched on the sofa's side table.

It had been a barefoot ceremony on a pristine Hawaiian beach. She was in a long dress with a free-flowing design of wild red Hawaiian orchids splashed across a purple background. Her short, black hair was even curlier than usual and it was topped with a crown of white plumeria. Harry wore a sky-blue silk shirt that made his eyes even bluer. His dark curly hair was flying with the wind. He was the most beautiful person she'd ever seen.

"You know, you've only been gone a day, but it feels like forever. I miss you so much."

"Me, too."

She scratched Tuva's neck again, then reached for the picture. She trailed a finger across his smiling face and sighed.

"How do you like the facility?"

"North Coast Hospital is a fairly small place and there's not a lot of action here right now, at least not for my taste. Actually,

28

it's not too far from Oceanview," Harry laughed. "Remember Oceanview with all that top- notch technology?"

"Robots and pregnancy. How could I forget?"

"It was there we found out all the doctors were wrong and that you *could* get pregnant with our Baby X."

Gina patted her tummy. "Only five months ago but I feel like I've been pregnant since the beginning of time." There was a long pause; she could hear him breathing and could tell they were both thinking about being apart.

Harry finally broke the silence. "I better go and grab some dinner before my break is up. Love you, doll."

"Love you, too."

* * *

Gina was in the kitchen when Helen rang the bell. She gave the sauce another quick stir with a wooden spoon, tasted it, and hurried to the door to let her best friend in. She looked through the peephole and flipped the deadbolt.

"Just me," Helen said. She propped her dripping umbrella against the outside wall and stepped inside.

"I don't take anything for granted anymore. Looking through a peephole is the least I can do to try to stay out of trouble." She helped Helen out of her raincoat. "Is it raining hard?"

"Hard enough."

"Here we are making small talk when all either of us wants to do is talk about Vinnie." Gina went into the kitchen and poured from Harry's open bottle of cabernet. She picked the glass up and handed it to Helen.

"Thanks. What are you having?"

"An exciting glass of milk, dontcha know?" She reached for the spoon and mixed the sauce again, then looked at her friend. "How are you doing?"

Helen took a sip of wine before answering.

"All those years when I was single, I was never lonely. Now, without Vinnie, I feel empty and disconnected." She gulped

29

down more wine. "And worried. Something inside is terrifying me, making me afraid I'll never see him again."

Gina grabbed Helen by the shoulders. "Don't say that. Don't even think it for one second."

"I can't help it."

"Helen, I heard from Pablo□".

Helen was stunned. "Does he know where Vinnie is?"

"He checked himself into Bone Point, that hospital where Guy died."

"Helen whirled around and started toward the door. "I've got to go to him. Now!"

"Stop! There's nothing you or any of us can do, right now."

"But I need to do *something*, Gina!"

"Think about it. At least we know where he is. He's safe. That's the most important thing."

The timer went off. Startled them.

Gina glanced at the boiling spaghetti, then at Helen. "Let's eat…slow things down and make a plan."

Helen responded with a reluctant nod, finished her wine, and refilled the glass.

"Grab the bread, please," Gina said as she divided the pasta onto the plates, then spooned out the thick sauce.

Helen sat down, dropped the napkin onto her lap and stared straight ahead.

"I slaved over a hot stove all day making that sauce. You *will* eat!" Gina pressed Helen's hand. "For me. Please."

Helen picked up a spoon and fork, twirled the spaghetti over and over, and finally took in a mouthful.

She smiled weakly at Gina. "This is really good."

"*Mangia. Mangia!*"

* * *

Helen had brought a couple of apple tarts. She and Gina sat in the living room with freshly brewed coffee and the desserts. She'd chosen the tarts because she knew Gina loved them. But now it was Gina who wasn't eating.

Helen asked, "Are *you* okay, Gina?"

"You know I'm not." Her dark eyes were intense. "We both need to know what's happening to Vinnie. Like you, I can't sit around and do nothing."

"So what are we going to do?"

"Just hear me out."

Helen had seen that look in her best friend's eyes before. She was up to something. When it came to Harry or her brother, there wasn't much she wouldn't do to protect them.

Helen watched her friend's hand shake as she drew the cup to her lips and sipped her coffee.

"I called Bone Point this afternoon to see if they were hiring nurses."

"What?" Helen could barely breathe. "No! Stop right now." She moved over and wrapped her arms around Gina. "No! You're not going to do this."

"I am." Gina gently pulled away. "He's my brother. I need to know if he's being treated right. I need to see him, get my hands on him, make sure he's not being abused."

Helen covered her face. "Oh, no. Please don't say that." She could feel a hole in her chest opening up ... inside, everything was dying.

"But you could lose your baby ... please, please, please don't do this." She was almost screaming when she said, "I'm an RN, too. *I'm* going, not you."

Gina took her hand. "You have a job to keep. And it's only going to be for a couple of days ... just so I can get inside that place and see what's happening. Mostly, they're looking for medication nurses. Not too much running around with that."

"I don't believe it. All we ever do is run."

"I'll be careful. I promise."

"The baby□"

"Stop with the baby crap, already. I have the time, you don't. This is a good plan."

"I still don't like it."

31

"Look, when I spoke to the nursing manager, she was anxious to interview me and have me start right away. I think they're having problems attracting RNs. They'd probably take on anyone willing to work there."

"It's not safe."

"It's only for a couple of days." Gina took a bite of her tart. "I only want to see Vinnie, get to the bottom of what the hell's going on with him, and bring him home."

"What if it's more than a couple of days?"

"It won't be." Gina smiled at her. "I'll keep in touch with Harry by cell phone and I'll be back before he gets home."

Helen knew she should call Harry right away, let him know what Gina was up to. This was dangerous for her pregnancy.

I know I should stop her.

But she just couldn't make herself do it.

Chapter 6

Wednesday Morning

Harry tossed and turned all night, unable to get comfortable in the North Coast Hospital bed. There was something about his conversation with Gina that was … off. He tried to chalk it up to stay-at-home restlessness and her worry about Vinnie. After a while, he was able to fall asleep. But a couple of hours later he woke up thinking about her again.

He tried to call her, but the call went straight to her message box.

Later, at work, he tried again, with the same result.

Anxious, he called Helen.

"Do you have a moment? I need to talk to you about our gal."

"Well, I'm kind of in the middle of things. Let me call you back in a few minutes … during my break."

He was busy at the computer, tapping in his nurses' notes, when she got in touch with him.

"Harry, what's the matter?"

"Look, I'm not trying to pry into your relationship with Gina, but I'm worried about her." He reached for a pad of paper and began to doodle. First he printed Gina's name in large script, then made swirls of elaborate ink scrolls around each letter.

Helen and Gina had been friends ever since she moved to California. They'd been through a lot together. Even Harry probably didn't know Gina as well as Helen did.

"What are you thinking of specifically?" Helen asked.

"This whole pregnancy has been really hard on her …no matter how much she wants it."

"Well, is it any wonder? Having to have her cervix stitched up and generally becoming a living incubator isn't much in the way of a life for someone like Gina."

"I got that ... believe me. I don't know how we're going to get through the next four months." He hesitated. "But right now, I think she's more worried about Vinnie than anything else."

"Well, Harry, get a grip." She sounded angry. "He's her brother and he's my fiancé. We're *both* going crazy."

"Hey, I know. I am, too. I probably shouldn't have taken this assignment when there's so much going on. Did she say anything last night when you were together?"

There was a long pause.

"Helen, are you there?"

"Yeah, I'm here ... we both talked about Vinnie. That's about all."

"Okay. You would tell me if there was anything I should know?" He crumpled the paper and threw it in the trash basket. "No secrets. Right?"

Was he imagining it or was Helen's laugh forced? "Have there ever been any secrets between the four of us?"

Answering his question with a question wasn't reassuring.

* * *

Gina packed enough clothes for the next few days at the VA hospital. The suitcase was filled mostly with scrubs. She slipped into her white work sneakers and checked her purse to make sure it held anything she might need: Swiss army knife, cell phone, wallet, Band-Aids, antihistamines, a large bottle of spring water, and the recently added pepper spray.

At the last minute, she left a message on Helen's cell, letting her know she was taking off for the VA hospital. She started to call Harry, but hesitated, and then decided to let it go. Lying really wasn't her thing.

After wheeling her small suitcase from the apartment, she shoved it into the passenger seat of the Fiat, then went around to the driver's side, and climbed in. She caressed the steering wheel for a moment hoping the car wouldn't get into one of its temperamental moods.

Be a good girl and behave yourself. Please. Just for me.

* * *

There had been dark clouds overhead when Gina left San Francisco. Now, under partly cloudy skies, she was driving north on a winding road that was surrounded by thick forests. It was fun to drive the Fiat, but it required all of her concentration not to misjudge a curve and end up smashed into a tree.

Her destination was definitely off the beaten path, which made her wonder why they would use a hospital so far from a large city population. But anything she knew about the VA had come strictly from Vinnie and Harry, and that wasn't much. She finally decided someone had to take care of veterans in Northern California beyond San Francisco. Maybe the decaying hospital was the most practical solution.

A few fat drops of rain fell on the windshield, but that was all. It didn't pour down as she had expected, and the weatherman had predicted.

Good thing Harry put the top up a few days ago before the rainy season started. I always hang up the damn vinyl on something.

She sang out loud, shattering the silence when she entered a radio dead zone. Thinking about the baby kept her optimistic for many miles, but the closer she got to her destination, the more Vinnie invaded her thoughts. That segued into fears that she could be risking the life of her unborn child. She dropped into silence and a sudden sense of dread made her slow down and twist in the driver's seat.

She needed to rethink what had sent her on this unscheduled journey.

What happened to Vinnie? Why did he take off like that? Was it really because Guy West was dead?

She couldn't imagine what he could accomplish by signing himself into an inpatient psych hospital that, according to his counselor Pablo, had a reputation of being a sewer drop.

Gina looked around at the tall pines. She hated this time of the year when the days grew shorter; it felt as though she was constantly surrounded by darkness.

The hospital finally came into view. It was only 3:00 P.M., but it felt much later. She pulled over to the side of the road to look at the building.

It was dead ahead.

Gloomy looking, it was perched on a spit of land that reached out onto a cliff, high above the ocean. Dark shadows surrounded massive white rocks and boulders of all sizes. It looked like broken bones were scattered everywhere.

The hair on Gina's arms rose.

Just then, her cell rang. It was Harry. She took a deep breath and answered.

"Hello, there."

"Hi, doll. How are you doing? I've tried to call a couple of times, but your phone was turned off."

She swallowed hard, trying to speak. This was the hardest part. Lying to Harry.

"I'm fine. I turned the phone off because I was getting string of robocalls and they were driving me nuts. Right now, I'm reading and doing nothing. How's the assignment going?"

"ICU is kind of quiet right now, if you can believe that … so I'm working in the ER."

"Only two more days … I just hate it when you're gone."

"So everything is okay?" He hesitated. "I don't know, you sounded kind of … different last night when we talked."

"You're just a worry wart. It's all good … but it would be a whole lot better if you were here."

"I know. So everything *is* okay?"

"You already asked me that. I'm just fine."

36

"Okay, doll. I gotta run. I'll talk to you tonight." Before she could respond, he said, "Hey, you! Stay out of trouble."

"*Moi?* she said with a chuckle that sounded hollow. "When have I ever gotten into trouble?"

"Let's not go there, babe." And *he* wasn't laughing.

Chapter 7

Wednesday, 3:00 pm

Delores Smiley hated being the nursing supervisor at Bone Point.

It was mostly a matter of respect. Even though her salary had been upped considerably a couple of years ago, and the juicy extracurricular work brought in a pretty penny, that did nothing for all the aggravation tossed her way, topped off with having to deal with crazy, drugged-up veterans.

Then there was the risk.

And our great administrator, Norman Glick? Not that it's the bastard's real name. It's actually Samish, just like all of my distant cousins from that side of the family. What a prick.

Every time she thought about their last conversation, she went ballistic. Norman had laughed in her face.

"Are you kidding me? *You* want more money? Your cut of the action gives you plenty of money. If you weren't my cousin you wouldn't even have a decent job."

"What do you mean by that, Norman?"

"I mean you'd been fired by three hospitals before we started working together closing VA hospitals. That's when you started making real money."

She'd gone silent, but that didn't stop him.

"Of course, none of those hospitals you worked for would say why they were killing a good referral. 'Cause that's the law … but it was pretty obvious that it had to be pretty damn damaging for you, smiley face, not that you've ever told me."

She ignored the dig. But he'd had the nerve to mess with her name, like she hadn't grown up with a thousand *cute* little remarks because her name was Smiley.

She shook off the memory, checked her schedule, and looked at her watch.

Where the hell is the new gal I hired over the phone?

Delores had been in and out of nursing for twenty-five years and she still couldn't believe how they did things today. Now she could check out a job applicant's history, grab any information she needed online, and then decide whether or not to hire the person.

It was amazing what she could find out. It gave her real choices.

Not that any nurse was banging down the door to work in this dump. In fact, getting even one to work here at all in this godforsaken place was a real nightmare. But at least checking online, this new nurse seemed very competent.

Delores would take her, no matter what. This place was way understaffed, even with only fifteen patients left. And closing up in two months isn't exactly attractive in the way of job security.

She tapped her pencil on the desk, getting more and more impatient as she checked her watch again. What if the nurse didn't show?

The dumbass orderlies did everything and anything, but the hospital still couldn't let those bozos give out meds. It was against the law and even if the administration tried, they'd never get away with it. Someone would sure as hell report them.

Besides, the RNs were the only licensed people they still had on staff since they lost their last in-house doc. There was no way they could rid of the few nurses they had left.

She rummaged through the papers on her desk, found what she was looking for: Gina Mazzio Lucke.

What the hell was this? Three names? No way. It was going to be either Mazzio or Lucke. Who does she think she is?

Cool it or you'll lose her, too, just like all the others.

She eyed her watch yet again and shifted in the chair. Gina What's-her-name was definitely supposed to be here by now.

I've set her up for the swing shift, which will be starting pretty darn quick, and I've got to hurry to electroconvulsive therapy. Fill in there.

It was exactly 3:30 when her phone buzzed. She pressed the speaker button.

"Hi, Ziggy. Please tell me you've got that new nurse we've been expecting there with you."

"Yes, ma'am. She's here right in front of me."

"Well, by all means, bring her in."

* * *

Gina wiped her sweaty palms on the sides of her scrub pants and clutched her jacket closed, trying to mask her pregnancy. She'd conveniently left out that fact from the form she filled out online.

Don't ask. Don't tell.

The receptionist had a worried look when she'd openly appraised Gina. There were questions in her soft brown eyes. Well, Gina had questions, too.

She followed the receptionist, whose nametag said she was Ziggy Jones.

As they walked down the hallway, Gina asked, "Do you like your job here?"

Ziggy's dark skin turned gray and she seemed to tighten up. "I guess I do."

They passed an oversized elevator, its door open. With a quick glance, Gina could see it was also used for carrying wheelchairs and gurneys; the side walls were scarred where metal equipment had slammed into them. Each step took her away from a whiff of something dirty inside the elevator. There'd been some kind of odor Gina couldn't identify. It was cloying and it made her feel sick.

"The Nursing Supervisor's office is down at the end of the hall."

Gina tried to walk abreast with the receptionist, but she obviously didn't want any more conversation. She made sure Gina stayed a few steps behind.

Jeez. Most people have to get to know me before they back off.

After tapping on a door etched with the pertinent info, Delores Smiley, Supervisor, Ziggy opened it without waiting and they walked into a small office that only had a desk and two chairs. It was the barest office Gina had ever been in.

The receptionist said, "Ms. Smiley, this is the nurse you've been waiting for."

"Thanks, Ziggy."

Without a word, Ziggy turned around, left, closing the office door a little harder than Gina would have expected.

"As Ziggy said, I'm Ms. Smiley … you must be Gina, right?"

Gina held out her hand, but the supervisor hesitated before barely grasping it.

"That's right."

"Have a seat, Ms. Mazzio. Or is it Lucke?"

Gina smiled. "I've recently gotten married and I love my new name, Lucke."

The supervisor had short frizzy hair and was probably somewhere in her fifties.

When Gina sat, she tried to keep her jacket closed. But it barely hid her baby bump.

"How many nurses on staff, Ms. Smiley?"

She looked at Gina with piercing eyes. "It seems you've gotten your role here reversed, Ms. Lucke. I'm asking the questions."

A fiery heat flushed Gina's face.

I wonder how such a dour woman could end up with the name Smiley.

"You're pregnant, aren't you?"

Gina's heart raced and she couldn't catch her breath. She nodded.

42

"Beggars can't be choosers." Smiley leaned back into her chair. "But you need to understand, if I can find a replacement … you're out of here."

"I understand," Gina said.

"Good. Now let's get going; I need you on duty as quickly as possible."

* * *

The elevator door clanked shut, locking in the unpleasant odor Gina had only caught a whiff of earlier. She and Dolores began a slow climb to the second floor.

"This building is over seventy years old and this elevator has been here since its beginnings."

"It does look rundown."

"It was built at the end of World War Two." Delores Smiley leaned against the back wall as the elevator jerked to a stop between floors. "Don't worry, she's an old lady … just resting until she starts pulling again."

"How do you know she'll start up?"

"Experience, Ms. Lucke."

Gina could feel the sweat dripping under her arms.

"Besides, repairs are few and far between because we'll be closing the hospital in the next two months. And sometime within the next few years the whole kit and caboodle's scheduled for demolition." The elevator jerked and started up again. "I've seen pictures of this place … what it looked like when it was new," the supervisor continued. "In nineteen forty-four, it was sparkling."

"Can't they update it … renovate it? Seems to me they don't have enough medical treatment places for vets the way it is."

"Way too expensive. Can't even sell the damn thing … too far from heavily populated areas. Right now most of our patients are psychiatric overflows from other VA hospitals … those who can't be treated in private clinics."

Gina breathed out as the doors creaked open.

"I don't have time for a formal orientation to the whole hospital, I'm only taking you to the unit where you'll be working."

"Okay."

"We'll work out your days off and other administrative details later," Delores Smiley said.

Gina, hoping to see Vinnie, scrutinized the face of every patient she saw shuffling down the hallway. One of the men fell against her, almost knocking her over. He looked bewildered. Gina took his arm and steadied him. "It's okay," she said to the patient.

The supervisor seemed to hardly notice. "Most of these patients are awaiting complete evaluation by our visiting psychiatric staff. That can take a while." She stopped, turned to look at Gina. "Pregnant or not, you'll be expected to tend to them when you're not giving meds. Do you understand?"

"Yes."

"Most of these men have severe PTSD and are heavily sedated, mainly so they don't hurt themselves. Do you know anything about PTSD, Ms. Lucke?"

"Yes, I've read a great deal about it."

"Good."

Farther down the hall, Gina saw Vinnie coming toward them, dragging one foot after the other. He was pale and his body moved as though his bones had melted. Each step seemed uncoordinated and painful.

Gina's breath caught in her throat. He looked sick and lost. When he was right in front of her, they looked into each other's eyes.

Vinnie, it's me.

He didn't seem to know that he was seeing his big sister.

She was crushed. All she wanted to do was hug him close, then grab his hand and run. When he looked at her with those vacant eyes, it was as though someone had pierced her soul and let all of her energy drain away.

Chapter 8

Thor watched the rat-faced supervisor bring in a new nurse.

So the rumors are true. Heard something about them snagging a new one. Hasn't been anyone hired in this dump for months. Hell, who wants to be workin' in a joint that's shutting down?

Thor checked out the merchandise from head to toe. He liked the look of her even if she was a mite too tall for his taste. He chuckled under his breath.

She won't seem that big layin' down with her legs spread.

As they moved closer, he frowned.

Fuck's sake. She's knocked up.

He was so busy staring at the nurse, he almost fell when one of the nut jobs walked right into him.

"Hey, you!" He elbowed the fool. "Do that again and I'll put you in a meat grinder, or maybe we'll tie ya down again. Remember that? We know how to make it even worse."

The fool ignored him. Thor grabbed him by the arm and squeezed as hard as he could.

"Look at me!"

The stupid zombie stared back at him in a funny way before his eyes went blank.

"Get moving, creep. Stay outta my way!"

Fucking unbelievable. Let lowlifes like that in the military but turn me down.

Eddie came out of a patient's room, pushing a laundry cart. "Hey, man. Don't just stand there. Get in that room and help clean up the mess. I'm not doing it by myself."

"You'll do it if I say so."

"The hell I will," Eddie said. "One day you're gonna get your ass handed to you, talkin' to me like that."

Thor wanted to laugh at him and the pissed look on his face.

"I don't take orders from you," Eddie said. He sneered at Thor then glanced at the supervisor and the new nurse. "Well, well. Lookee here." He nodded toward the two women. They were moving in his direction, probably to the nurses' station. "She's a really good looker even if she is knocked up."

"Don't bother me none," Thor said.

Eddie laughed. "Same here."

* * *

Gina and Delores approached the two orderlies standing in the hallway. Gina had watched a patient slam into one of them; her stomach turned when she saw the orderly rough him up.

Stop it! Stop hurting him.

She swallowed hard and turned to Delores. "Do the orderlies always push the patients around like that?" She indicated the patient being manhandled.

That bastard will pay.

"Oh, that! You'll learn to ignore the small stuff or you'll be the one cleaning up patient messes … instead of them doing it."

The supervisor stopped in front of the two orderlies. "Thor, Eddie, I want you to meet our new medication nurse, Gina Lucke." She pointed a finger at them. "Now you behave and be nice to her."

"Yes, ma'am," they both said.

She nodded at the orderlies and followed Delores to the glass-enclosed nurses' station. There was a barred, teller-like window, behind which a nurse, somewhere in her late fifties, sat watching them. It wasn't hard to see she was ticked off. She unlocked the door to the station and they walked inside. Delores locked the door behind them.

"This is Lena Rossner, our day-shift RN. She covers new admissions and patients waiting for evaluation, and of course hands out meds." As they were shaking hands, the supervisor continued, "Lena, meet Gina Lucke. She'll be the swing shift med nurse."

"Nice to meet you. Sorry, but I have to fly. I'm already late for an appointment."

Gina watched the short, overweight woman grab her purse and hurry out of the station. Delores locked the door behind her.

"We have tight security here. This is where all the immediate drugs and other equipment are kept."

"I see."

"No, I don't think you do. You're a babe in the woods here." She put the crowded key ring back into her pocket. "When was the last time you worked in a psych unit?" She paused. "Never mind!" She waved a hand. "I know from your resume you never have. So you have a lot to learn."

"I'm sure I do."

Gina looked back down the hallway but Vinnie was gone. And she hadn't seen which room he disappeared into.

"Do you have a nurses' Kardex?" Gina asked. "I'm used to working with them. It's helpful for getting to know the individual patients and their needs. "

"The computer will give you everything you need to know about each vet." Delores frowned at her. "None of the nurses want to bother with a unit card file."

Gina nodded, trying to control her temper.

"Why would you need individual Kardex information, anyway? Everyone gets meds the minute they're admitted. That's what *you're* here for. Nothing changes until their psych evaluation is completed."

Gina was becoming restless and angry. "Don't you think I need to know more about these men … my patients? They're not just room numbers. Shouldn't I at least know their names … have a hint of their individual problems? A unit Kardex is fast and crucial." Gina couldn't stop herself. "And how long is it before these men are evaluated?"

Delores looked sharply at her. "Are you trying to make some kind of statement, nurse? Because that's not what you're here for."

Gina forced herself to smile, but she wasn't going to let it go.

"It's only a simple question," Gina said. "How long do they have to wait before they're evaluated?"

"On average, it takes a month ... sometimes two."

"But what if they need immediate treatment?" Gina's stomach was churning.

"Cut the attitude right now or you're out the door before you even start. Our standing orders and protocols cover all temporary situations."

With that, Delores pulled another key ring out of her pocket. This one had fewer keys on it. One by one she showed Gina what each key was for, then gave her the key ring. Labels were on every key. One said, Tunnel.

Gina held it up to Delores. "Tunnel?"

"It's the bottom floor at Bone Point." She pulled out a rolling desk chair and sat. Gina did the same. "The kitchen, morgue, a small lab, some treatment areas, our electroconvulsive therapy area and a lot of empty rooms are down there."

"Well, isn't that cozy," Gina said, laughing.

"Cozy? I doubt you'll think so when you have to go down there."

* * *

Vinnie sat down on his bed, his heart racing. He was swimming in sweat. He covered his face, trying to get himself together.

Why is Gina here? She'll only get in trouble. And her baby? What's going to happen to it? She's supposed to be on bed rest.

He felt sick. He swallowed repeatedly, trying to keep from throwing up.

I'm such a fool. What have I done? I should have known she'd find a way to track me down.

Vinnie looked at Dallas Dacy, the vet in the bed next to his.

"Hey, man, what's biting your ass?" Dallas said.

"I don't like that creep, Thor."

"Welcome to the club." Dallas looked at him with clear eyes.

Vinnie noticed the vet didn't seem to feel the shitload of drugs they were all forced to take.

"How come you don't zone out on all those pills?" Vinnie asked.

Dallas turned away from him. "That's on a need-to-know basis."

"Oh, yeah? So if you tell me, you'll have to kill me."

Dallas turned away. He wasn't laughing.

* * *

Vinnie remembered his first full day here. It felt like he'd been here for months even though it was less than two days ago.

Standing in front of the nurses station window, the day nurse, Lena, had tapped her finger on the counter ... waiting.

"Either swallow those pills right in front of me, or you'll end up in restraints," she said in a calm, unemotional voice. "Why make it tough on yourself? You're going to take them one way or the other ... like it or not. Heck, just do it."

He'd stood there staring at her.

"Listen, soldier, it's no skin off my nose."

"It's *marine,* ma'am." He grabbed the small paper medicine cup filled with pills and tossed them on the floor, then stomped them.

The nurse shook her head and nonchalantly tapped a bell on the counter. It seemed like only a moment before Thor and Eddie were on either side of him.

The nurse said, "He's not in the mood to take his pills. Maybe you can help change his mind."

He tried to fight them off, but in the end they dragged him down to the end of the hall, took him into an empty room, and slammed the door shut. There was nothing in there except a grungy, torn, sheetless gurney. He felt sick when he saw the leather bindings attached to the side rails

"Strip!" Eddie said.

49

"No way. Let's go back. I'll take the damn pills."

"You bet your ass you will," Thor said with a smirk. "But only when we're good and ready to take you back to get them."

"Come on, guys. I said I'd take them."

They picked him up and tossed him onto the gurney. Before he could even resist, they strapped his wrists down. He kicked at each of them and his heel hit Thor's chest.

Thor moved in and slugged him. A flash of lightning tore through his head. That's all he remembered before he passed out.

When he awoke he was naked and strapped to the table. The room was pitch black and he was disoriented, soaking wet in his own urine.

"Hey!" he screamed into the silence. "I'll take the fucking pills. Let me out of here!"

Panic gripped him. He was panting and could barely breathe. He knew he was going to die. They were going to kill him. He yanked at the straps until he thought his wrists would snap.

"Let me out! Let me out! Let me out!"

When they finally came for him, he was still screaming.

* * *

After Gina was told where the drugs were kept and given a quick look at the narcotics, Delores told her she was on her own.

"If you get hungry, there are vending machines on the first floor in the break room. We no long have a functioning kitchen. All patient meals are brought in from the outside."

Without further explanation, she turned and left.

All Gina could think about was getting back on the elevator and flying out the front door. Instead, she looked around the station and swallowed down her feelings of being trapped.

She wasn't going anywhere without her brother.

Before getting started on the medications, she placed her fingers on her pulse and felt the pounding rhythm rush over her. It soothed her with its steadiness. She patted her belly.

No pain, no discomfort. I'm good to go. You hang in there, kid.

Noises started getting through. Patients were milling around the window and she realized she'd better get going. Each med cup was placed on a of 2x2 doctor's medicine-order card; each had the patient's name, drug, and delivery times.

She was late distributing the 4:00 p.m. meds and needed to attend to those right away. It looked like an awful lot of medicine cards for a unit with only fifteen patients.

She quickly riffled through the stack and found her brother's medicine card: Clonazepam 1 mg daily.

Wait a minute!

She'd done some preliminary research on the PTSD drugs they might treat Vinnie with. She brought his record up on the computer.

Yes, he was getting Zoloft, an antidepressant. She knew it would increase his serotonin levels to try to improve his moods. But they were also giving him both Hydrocodone with Clonazepam to cut down on sleep arousal. It was a heavy duty combination that seemed wrong and dangerous. Especially since they hadn't even evaluated him.

Vinnie was being zonked out.

Is this how they control the patient population? Makes them compliant?

"Hey, nurse. When do we get our meds?"

The patients were at the window, glaring at her.

She quickly lined up the medication cups. Her hands shook as she started filling them.

Chapter 9

Delores Smiley tore out of the ECT treatment room, where they were using electricity to cause a seizure in a depressed patient. The only result Delores saw, time and time again, was a jumbled, confused brain.

Tears stung her eyes. Visions of her dead husband haunted her.

Watching someone's brain explode in an electrical fury from 450 volts, even in a controlled environment, destroyed every reason she had for becoming a nurse. It was barbaric.

Gary died from those seizures. Oh, not right away. But after weeks of those *treatments* he turned into an apathetic, indifferent lump. It didn't matter what the doctors said or claimed. That's what happened.

Her stomach turned as she hurried down the corridor. Today was the anniversary of his death. He'd been gone for ten years.

Ten whole years!

She wiped the tears from her eyes, couldn't stand to wait for the elevator. She flung open the exit door and took the steps two at a time. She pulled hard on the railing, yanking herself upward, not daring to stop until she reached her apartment on the fourth floor.

When Norman Glick first took control of Bone Point, he had suggested she move to the deserted floor, just as he had. It not only saved money, it kept them right on top of the progressive shutdown of the hospital.

But today, as she hurried up the stairs, her head was filled only with thoughts of her deceased husband.

She pictured Gary's face: chiseled features that looked as though they were cut from hard-chipped granite. Yet his large green eyes could see deep into her soul.

He was a career soldier, just like her father. But her father had come through Vietnam unscathed and proud, even when the population was spitting on him and other vets every chance they got. But Gary had been crushed by his service. He'd survived in body, but what came back wasn't her Gary anymore.

All he wanted to do was die.

She desperately tried to get him into VA treatment programs, but the waiting period was more than a year everywhere she turned. She dragged him off to private treatment centers where they filled him with packets of drugs and finally killed his brain with ECT. Instead of getting better, he became more and more distant, more listless.

Then one day he just walked away and became one of the lost ones.

A private detective took five months to finally track him down, stuffed into a sleeping bag in a San Francisco alley. She got him into a VA hospital that was similar to Bone Point.

At her room, she unlocked the door and edged inside, threw the ring of keys on a cheap dresser.

For some reason, the new nurse popped into her head.

Idealistic, patient oriented, and pregnant to boot. Well, who cares what she or anyone else says? All a lot of talk.

The supervisor covered her face. She was still shaken by the ECT treatment and what had happened to her husband.

When Gary died from a cocktail of pills and gin, she dropped out of everything for a full year. During that time, an inferno of fury kept building inside of her. Yes, she was angry. Furious at the whole system and not in the way this new nurse was.

Idealism wasn't going to change anything. Only stripping the bureaucracy of its power would alter the equation. She would help destroy that system.

One that ignored her Gary.

One that made promises it couldn't keep.

Gary had served his country, but when he came home, the system turned its back on him.

She knew veterans needed to become disillusioned and angry, come out from everywhere in the country, descend on Washington, and destroy a heartless bureaucratic system.

Bone Point was going to close. No different than the last two facilities Norman and Delores shut down. Yes, the two of them were brought in to improve hospital services. But, with poor oversight, they allowed things to get worse. Inefficient, poorly run hospitals were considered a waste of money and were soon closed.

Norman was happy. He was making tons of money and not just from the hospital. And it all suited Delores's plan, too

Only when there were no more places for vets to go, no more drugs for them to take, no more streets for them to lie on, would they finally stand up and fight for their lives and the protection they deserved.

For now, all of them were damaged, afraid, and useless.

* * *

Donnie watched the nurse with the frizzy hair from a closet in the tunnel, watched her run from the scary room. She hurried up the stairs and he wanted to run after her and grab her, tell her to leave. No one was safe here. But he wasn't ready to come out of his hiding place.

The hermit had lots of hiding places to escape the world.

That's how he liked to think of himself.

A hermit.

No one except Ziggy knew he could melt through the walls of the Tunnel, or that he lived on the fifth floor in a dark, dark space filled with lost memories.

No one.

Chapter 10

Wednesday, 11:30 pm

Gina stood at the entrance where the hospital lights highlighted sheets of continuous rain, dousing an already soggy landscape. There were huge puddles of water all over the parking lot.

Good thing I parked in the covered part of their lot. My Fiat would have drowned in this downpour.

She was surprised to see Delores coming toward her, looking like she'd been walking in the rain for quite some time. Her hair and raincoat were drenched.

"You're out late," Gina said.

Delores ignored the remark and said, "How was your first day, Gina?"

If you must know, it was the most horrible shift of my life.

"It was different."

The supervisor gave her a weak smile. "I'll bet." She laid a hand on her arm. "It's really late, Gina. I suggest you stay in one of the fourth-floor rooms."

"Well, I don't know☐"

"Don't be silly. Look, you don't live nearby … where are you going to go at this time of night?"

"I already have a reservation at a nearby motel … The Sleep Over."

"That rundown place? No way. We have rooms on the fourth floor, stay there tonight."

"But my clothes…"

"Plenty of time for that tomorrow … maybe it will have stopped raining."

The supervisor seemed different tonight. Her eyes were red-rimmed and her shoulders drooped. Not the haughty person she'd been when Gina first met her at the beginning of the swing shift.

It had been a weird evening. After spotting Vinnie in the hallway, she'd tried to track him down on and off throughout the day without any luck. It was as though he was deliberately avoiding her.

Would he do that to me?

They'd always been so close. She thought she knew him even better than Harry. Could she have been that wrong about coming here?

No. Something was definitely wrong with him ... wrong with this place.

Why would he drop everything, leave Helen, and take off? Nothing was going to bring Guy West back. He was dead.

Vinnie needs to get out of here. Back home to us.

She'd closely watched the two orderlies who worked the second floor. They had yes-ma'am-ed, no-ma'am-ed her the whole shift. But their treatment of the patients, the way they pushed them around, held an undercurrent of predatory nastiness. And these poor vets were so zoned out they didn't seem to notice.

Ugh. I have to get away from those orderlies with their creepy eyes crawling up and down my body.

But she was so exhausted she couldn't think about it anymore. Every muscle in her body ached and pulled her down.

She'd come to bring her brother home, but she hadn't done anything but wear herself out.

They stepped into the smelly elevator and Delores pressed the button for the fourth floor.

"What's on the third floor?"

"That's where we keep outdated equipment, old hospital beds, and furniture. Patients used to occupy all of the floors ... now they only occupy the second floor."

When they stepped out of the elevator, Gina could see a corridor full of guest rooms, most of the doors were open and the rooms unoccupied. In the long, dimly lit hall, the air felt heavy with that black gloom that seemed to be everywhere she looked. It was overtaking all of the old building.

"I thought this was a five-story building."

"Yes," Delores said. "That's right, but that floor was for female vets. It was the first area that we shut down in preparation for total closure."

"Closure?" she said, intentionally not letting on she already knew about it. Maybe Delores might slip her information Vinnie was looking for.

The supervisor stopped, looked at her. "You knew we were closing Bone Point. I mentioned it when you checked in?"

"I guess it didn't really sink in," Gina said.

"Yes, in two months or so this place will shut down for good."

"What happens to the patients here?"

"They'll be moved to other facilities or discharged." Delores was answering her questions but it was plain to see her mind was on something else.

She moved them along until they were standing outside one of the rooms. Its door was ajar. "You can stay here. I'm right down the hallway." She pointed to a door close by.

They walked inside the room. There was one bed in a space that could have held four. The air was heavy and stale. But more than that, a distinctive stink of fear tainted the atmosphere. The same odor she'd been aware of from the first moment she'd entered the building.

When she said goodnight, she locked the door … and wedged a chair under the doorknob.

While she was checking out the small bathroom, her phone rang.

"Why haven't you answered your phone, Gina?" Harry said, sounding frantic. "I've been worried to death about you." Gina looked at her watch: midnight.

I really messed up this time.

"Harry, I've been napping on and off the whole day. I'm so sorry."

"Sorry? And that's going to do it for you? Well, not for me."

"I was just going to call you. Please forgive me."

"Not this time."

"It's been an off day for me."

She knew he was fuming. He hung up on her.

* * *

This woman on the phone wasn't *his* Gina.

His Gina was an in-your-face kind of person who would hit you over the head with the truth, whether you wanted to hear it or not. Something's wrong.

She was lying to him. He was sure of it.

Harry had only two more days to cover ICU in Santa Cruz, but he'd be damned if he was going to let this roll off his back and wait it out.

Chapter 11

Thursday, 2:00 am

Through a hole in the floor, Donnie watched the new nurse sleep. Even from where he sat he could see darkness under her eyes. She was still pretty, with silky smooth skin and full lips. He wondered why she hadn't changed out of her scrubs.

He'd made a hole that went through the fifth floor to the room below. It had taken him a long time to do it with only a screwdriver, but it was the only tool he had and he couldn't make too much noise or *they* would find him.

It was right in that room below that he'd watched and listened to the hospital's man in charge talk to a scar-faced person about pills and things. The men stayed in the room for a while; the hermit listened, trying to make sense of what the two of them were saying. But they talked way too fast and he couldn't understand all the words.

He looked down below again. The bathroom light glowed on the nurse's face. He was drawn to her.

He hadn't been with a woman for years. Even the scattered dreams he used to have about being with a girl had stopped. Now, all he thought about was seeing his mother again.

When he closed his eyes to sleep, there was only a blank wall of nothingness. It had been that way since they stole his thoughts in that ugly room in the Tunnel.

After that he ran away and hid in the woods where it was quiet. The explosions and guns firing off in his head stopped. So did the sudden large globs of blood he used to see blossoming on his skin.

They were gone, too.

Bette Golden Lamb & J. J. Lamb

Then one night he got so hungry that he sneaked back into the hospital.

No one ever caught him, so he stayed. He'd been safe being a hermit since then, living in the hospital's shadows on the deserted fifth floor. And he'd come to love the darkness. That's why he liked it here. It was quiet without confusing voices to make his brain hurt.

He strained again to look closer at the nurse lying in her bed.

Once, a long time ago, he'd had his own woman. She was beautiful, too. Then, when he was away fighting, a car squashed her dead.

His insides felt weak trying to remember her.

He wiped at his wet cheeks.

I wanted to die, too.

But bombs or bullets never found him, even though he'd walk out in the middle of a battle field until the others would drag him back screaming.

They finally took him away from the war and sent him here, where they did terrible things to his brain. Everything got quieter, but he still thought about his woman, his mother.

His head was suddenly heavy and his eyes were trying to close. It took him several moments to get up and turn back into the silent shadows where he belonged.

* * *

Ziggy Jones avoided discussing her work at the hospital, even though her husband always had a lot of questions regarding the details of her job at Bone Point.

It kept her awake at nights, like last night, wondering what Fred was going to say when the news of the hospital's closure leaked out. He knew it was going to close *sometime*. Everyone from around here knew that. But now Ziggy really *knew* it would all be over in just two months, three at the most.

Fred had recently become a real estate agent and they were on shaky financial ground until he moved more homes. They needed her steady income and they wanted to start a family.

62

Although she never said it out loud, at thirty-seven she was getting long in the tooth that's what her mother called it. If they didn't have a baby in the next few years, it would be too late.

But if she couldn't work, they'd really be facing hard times. Ziggy never did well with just scraping by. When she'd found out that Bone Point was closing, she'd started looking for a new government job.

After filling out a request for a transfer within the VA's Department of Veterans Affairs, she was approached by an agent of the Inspector General's office. Ziggy was offered money to report on any irregularities at Bone Point and there was also the promise of a new job once the facility was closed down.

Now, she turned over again and again, trying to get comfortable, but her eyes remained wide open. Her thoughts shifted to the new nurse.

Might as well get up.

She slipped out of bed, trying not to disturb Fred, used the bathroom, and got dressed.

Ziggy couldn't help it. Pangs of jealousy had unsettled her the minute she met the RN. It seemed everyone was going to be a mother except Ziggy.

What was that nurse doing here? Why would any RN want to work in rundown, about-to-close hospital?

* * *

Dallas Dacy turned his head to look at Vinnie Mazzio. In the dim, early-morning light, Vinnie's eyes were smudges of black ink. Dallas hadn't made up his mind about the guy. Making friends was a dangerous prospect. The minute people got to know you, they wanted something from you. If you didn't give it to them, they'd find a way to screw you over.

Nope. Dallas would stay loose and unattached. This was a cushy place to lay his head down. He had no plans for living back on the streets of San Francisco … ever.

Chapter 12

Thursday, 6:00 am

Allison York arrived at her office a couple of hours earlier than normal. She listened very carefully to a recording of a paid informant giving her new information about the Bone Point Psychiatric Hospital. She was in the final stages of her investigation into the facility, and was anxious to have everything in order.

She stared down at the lettering on the identification card she wore on the pocket of her blouse:

Special Agent Allison York
OFFICE OF THE INSPECTOR GENERAL
U.S. DEPARTMENT OF VETERANS AFFAIRS

She was relatively new to the department, but she was a dedicated agent and her hard work had moved her through the ranks very quickly. She initiated this investigation three months ago after having approached the informant at the other end of this most recent recorded telephone conversation:

> *"You say they continue to admit veterans for treatment, even with a closure date in approximately three months?"*
>
> *"Yes. I've admitted two new walk-in patients very recently. Please, you've got to do something or more vets are going to die."*
>
> *"We're doing all that we can, but we can't just suddenly appear. It wouldn't get us anywhere. Believe*

me, we're auditing the records to verify the information you've been giving us."
"I'm doing the best that I can to help."

Allison had spoken with assurance, trying to calm the informant:

"I know that ... it's not your fault we haven't moved on this yet. We're working on it, but everything has to be bulletproof."

When she turned off the tape, her stomach was starting to cramp from the tension. Her insecurities were kicking in big time. She couldn't afford to screw up right from the start or her career could be over.

She'd gone through all the preliminaries of the Criminal Investigator Academy and she knew she was qualified for the job, but if she messed up it would be more than a career failure. It would end up a huge slap in the face for her brother's memory. He was the reason she became an agent in the first place.

He'd done two deployments in Afghanistan and when he came back the second time, he was a different man. Her mother and father had done all that they could to try to help him recover. But he'd brought the horrors of the war back with him and they tore him apart.

She thought of their last time together when he was still alive.

* * *

Allison had run into her brother's bedroom. He was screaming at the top of his lungs: "Fire! Fire! Fire!"

He never said anything else, he just kept screaming, "Fire! Fire! Fire!"

There was terror in his voice; his eyes bulged, drool ran down his chin, hands held an imaginary rifle: "Fire! Fire! Fire!"

She was in her last month of college, looking forward to her BA in philosophy. Until that moment she'd been a lighthearted, optimistic person.

But everything changed when he hanged himself. Yes. Her brother hanged himself.

She couldn't help it. She knew she'd let him down. Even a year of therapy never changed her opinion. It was her fault he was dead.

* * *

Allison pulled up her files on Bone Point Hospital.

Her notes read:

> *Ghosting patients?*
> *Stealing drugs?*
> *Stealing benefits?*
> *Physical abuse?*
> *Understaffing?*
> *Murder?*

Allison wasn't naïve, but could they get away with all of this?

Whenever she doubted any of this could happen in a licensed hospital, she heard her dead brother yelling, "Fire! Fire! Fire!"

Chapter 13

Thursday, 6:00 am

Gina awakened with a start. She was still in her scrubs, sprawled on top of a musty-smelling hospital bed.

She looked around, disoriented for a second. It was unsettling to wake up in a strange room, especially since she was shaking so hard she thought her chattering teeth would splinter.

She turned on her side and hugged herself until she stopped shivering.

I need to change out of these grubby clothes.

Earlier, she had rejected the idea of running out to the car in the rain to get her suitcase. Now she was sorry she hadn't gone. She was stuck wearing these rank things until morning.

The light was on in the bathroom, causing deep shadows that hid most of the room. There wasn't much to see anyway. Nothing but a windowless area with a single bed and a chair. It was like an upgraded cell.

Harry, you've married an idiot.

She had called Harry back right after he hung up on her. He was still fuming. He would barely talk to her.

"What are you up to, Gina?"

"Nothing, Harry."

"Are you lying to me?"

"I'm resting the best I can. Isn't that what you wanted?"

"What *I* wanted? What about you?"

"Yes, of course. Me, too." She paused. "Harry, I am taking care of myself." Then she was angry. "Did you think when I got pregnant I would give up who I am."

"I never thought that. I love you the way you are, but you can be reckless at times." He stopped a moment. "Right now, that's not an option."

"Harry, as I told you, I'm doing the best that I can."

"Damn, I should have never taken this assignment in Santa Cruz. I may bug out of here for the next two days. All I do is worry about you all the time."

"Harry, please don't do that. I'm pregnant, not dying. And you can't just come home. We both know you need to stay and finish your contract. Hell, it's only two more days."

There was a long pause. "I just want you to be safe."

"I know that. But I can take care of myself."

"Of course you can. That's not the point … I just don't want anything bad to happen to you."

"Harry, please stop worrying."

"Not an easy thing to do, Gina."

"Can't you believe me when I say I'm trying."

She'd hung up without really lying to him, but she wasn't telling him the truth, either. He would be furious if he knew what she was up to.

Now, she pushed off the bed, slipped on her shoes. When she stood, her legs were weak. She wobbled into the john and looked at her watch in the glow of the bathroom light.

Six o'clock!

She splashed warm water on her face. It felt so good that she ran her hands back and forth under the faucet for a few minutes. Finally, she moved to the door, set aside the chair propped under the doorknob, and stepped out.

Down the corridor everything looked creepy. There were only a few dim lights spaced along the hallway.

Looking at a shadowy figure, she jumped back. "What's that?" she said under her breath. The hair on her arms was standing up.

For a long moment it looked as if weird shadows were moving in different directions. She blinked hard and covered her eyes. When she opened them again, everything seemed normal.

Scary place.

She was shaking. She balled her fists and hurried until she was at the stairwell. Her fingers grasped the rail and she moved slowly down the two flights to the second floor. She peeked from the cracked open door into a dimly lit hallway.

The light was probably coming from the nurses station, which was just out of view. It all looked different than in the daytime. It confused her for a moment.

Getting her bearings, she hugged herself and hurried to the room the computer had said was supposed to be Vinnie's. She quietly slipped inside. It was pitch black. She'd barely closed the door when sharp fingernails stabbed into her arm and a hand covered her mouth. She tried to scream. She yanked hard at the fingers.

"Gina, it's me. It's okay."

Vinnie?

She thought she would faint as she held onto him. "Oh, my god, you're okay?"

"Raised in the Bronx and you think *this* is something?"

She knew he was bluffing.

"Why did you run away from home like that, Vinnie? We've been frantic with worry about you. We need to get you out of here right now."

"You know damn well why I'm here; I'm not going ... anywhere. The point is *you* have ... no business being here." He stopped to take a breath.

Vinnie's voice was sluggish. He sounded doped up.

"All right, you two," someone said. "That's enough. Ya hear me? Just shut the fuck up! How's a guy supposed to get any sleep with the two of you yammering away?"

"Hey, man ... sorry to wake you." Vinnie took Gina's hand. "Gina, this is Dallas Dacy; Dallas, this is my sister□"

"Yeah, I know. Gina … right?"

"I'm afraid we're going to wake up Rick," Vinnie said.

"Hey, dude, you should know better than that. The crap they give those vets will keep them under until much later." Dallas chuckled. "And with that empty vodka bottle under the bed, Rick is probably comatose."

"Gina, you need to go home … right now."

Her eyes had adjusted to the darkness and she could make out the outlines of Vinnie and Dallas. "I'm not going anywhere without you."

"I have to stay … I need to know what happened to Guy. How did he die?"

"You may not like what you find." Dallas's voice was harsh.

"If you know something, tell me. Either way, *I* have to know." Vinnie's voice had dropped to a whisper.

"Listen up," Dallas said. "Gina, get into the bathroom and close the door."

She just stood there.

"Now!"

Gina slipped into the bathroom.

The room door must have swung open. She could hear the night nurse talking.

"What's going on in here? Why are the two of you awake at this hour of the morning?" The nurse's voice became sterner. "This is unacceptable."

"I had a nightmare," Vinnie said. "Dallas was helping me."

Gina could see the flash of her Maglite sweep under the crack at the bottom of the door.

"Maybe we ought to give you both something to help you get back to sleep. We can't have you up crashing around. It's a good thing the other patient is not awake."

"I'm good," Vinnie said.

Then Dallas followed with, "No thanks. I'm good, too."

There was a long pause before the nurse said, "Okay, but I don't want to have to come here again. Get it!"

Minutes later, Vinnie opened the door, looked outside, and whispered, "It's clear, come on out."

"How did you know the nurse was there?" Gina said. "I didn't hear anything."

Dallas said, "Stay here long enough and you can hear a mouse crap three doors down."

"Come on, man," Vinnie said. "Is there anything you can help us with?" Vinnie asked.

"Look, you two." Dallas said. "I've got a sweet deal here … at least until they board up the place." His voice was low and mean. "I'm not risking anything just so you can find out what happened to a dead man."

"If this place is the reason Guy's dead, they can mess you up, too." Vinnie's voice was harsh.

"Leave me out of it. Got that?" Dallas's voice faded as he turned on his side away from them. "It's a shitty world out there and I don't want to go back before I have to.

* * *

Rick Bell listened to Vinnie, Vinnie's sister and Dallas whisper back and forth. It was hard to stay awake or concentrate on their words because his head was spinning every time he moved. But he knew they were up to something.

Well, who gives a fuck anyway.

All he needed was one more thing to mess him up. It was bad enough the sounds in his head never seemed to stop and lately he was sure he'd seen some creature wandering the halls in the middle of the night. He'd almost reported it to the nurse, but they'd want to know what he was doing up when he should be in bed.

Probably his imagination anyway. But things were starting to get more and more fuzzy and everything made less sense. He couldn't help but wonder why.

He reached under bed, pulled out a bottle of vodka and took two swigs. Soon it shut down all his thoughts and he was drifting off to sleep.

Bette Golden Lamb & J. J. Lamb

74

Chapter 14

Thursday, Earlier

Norman Glick pressed the elevator's down button. As he waited for it to chug up to the fourth floor, he pocketed his keys and looked back at the door to his private quarters. His eyes wandered a little farther down the hall to Delores Smiley's apartment. Both had been created years ago, a perk to entice administrative personnel to work for the hospital in its rural locale. It wasn't a much of a perk, as those things went, but it was something.

A good three minutes later the elevator doors clunked open.

Inside, he pressed the Tunnel button and the old elevator started its descent. He was used to the rattle that accompanied the ride and it didn't seem to matter whether it was straining to go up or coasting down. It sounded exactly the same: an expiring asthmatic.

Norman was tired and a little restless tonight. Well, really morning. Four in the morning.

He rarely had a good night's sleep anymore. Not since he was told months ago that Bone Point was closing within the next three months, even though the goal was in two months.

All the vets here would be dead or transferred. There'd be no more service in this northern part of the state. He knew he was in for a record-setting nightmare to make sure everything looked square. It was always the hardest part. But he'd made it work before and he would this time, too.

Where were they going to send a few of the remaining sick vets?

An unwanted feeling of pity made him shift from one foot to another.

I must be getting old, getting soft.

He hadn't become an administrator to help anyone, military or civilians.

When he was assigned to this rundown place, he'd wanted to pull his hair out. He felt like a loser. This was the worst of the three that had been targeted for closure. Who'd want to work in a wreck like this? But in the end it had turned out pretty good.

Today, it seemed the elevator thought the trip down to the Tunnel required resting at every floor before continuing the journey.

But it gave him time to think.

He knew vets everywhere were getting a bum deal. And no matter how hard he tried not to think about it, it bothered him every now and then. The things he'd done niggled at him. But it was a dog-eat-dog world. Why should he be his brother's keeper? Heck, he didn't even have anything to do with his biological brother, why would he want to take care of perfect strangers?

He'd milked the government dry with his under-the-table operations and had brought in millions of dollars that had swelled his bank accounts. That's all that mattered. He had to take care of number one.

But Manky Olav was really going to be pissed off with him this time. Norman should have never gotten involved with him.

He visualized the Russian sitting in his private Marin compound dressed in a custom-tailored suit. That's what he'd worn the last time Norman saw him.

Norman knew those rags had cost a fortune.

Did anyone still wear cufflinks? Manky did. Solid gold, along with a matching tie clip. Manky looked like a stylish Wall Street entrepreneur, not anything like what he really was a thug. No different than that scarred-up *associate* he sent once. Only once. Norman refused to deal with that man again.

Underneath the clothes, Norman knew Manky was a mass of bulging muscles. He'd seen firsthand. The two of them had done a steam bath together.

Only once.

Norman's flaccid body couldn't take that much negative self-shaming.

The administrator was restless even thinking about Manky.

When Norman finally got to the Tunnel, he stepped out of the elevator and moved down the dimly lit hallway.

This basement floor of the hospital was creepy in the daytime. At night, it was downright frightening. Even the kitchen at the other end of the long hallway was silent. The breakfast meal delivery wasn't due for another hour.

He passed the ECT area. It looked ghostly in the muted light. He stopped and looked into the room with all its monitors. Just the thought of having electricity course through your brain scared him. A procedure like that could make you crazy.

He stepped back and moved on past an empty room that held broken beds and outdated tech equipment. They should have been taken to the third floor, but never were.

Next came the morgue.

And the final room was a special patient holding area; there was no one waiting for a corpse pickup right now. He looked in at the six neatly made beds. All empty.

Norman picked up the pace as he passed.

At the very end were two large storage rooms. He looked around to make sure no one was following him, even though he knew no one else was around. The only footsteps he'd heard were his own.

He stood in front of the nearest door and entered codes into two separate electronic locks guarding the entrance.

No one was getting in there but him. When he opened the door, he felt himself flush.

Inside were shelves, filled from the floor to the ceiling with large stacked bottles of Vicodin, Klonopin, and morphine. Those were the top products, but there were also shelves stacked with Zoloft, and Seraquel. It always overwhelmed him to see this mammoth haul of drugs. And the other room was equally filled.

Manky would love Norman even with the next two reduced deliveries.

After that?

Visions of Hawaiian beaches floated through his mind. He wondered if he'd like island life.

* * *

Thor and Eddie stood at the staircase door … listening. Eddie was holding his breath, afraid to breathe.

"I told you."

"Man, what's the fool up to?" Eddy said.

"I'd bet my last dollar, he's stashed away a shitload of drugs," Thor said with a smirk. "Why else would he have two electronic entry codes for each of those rooms? Remember, I've been following him. I checked this out before."

"Yeah. What else could there be to steal from this joint?"

"Hell, why should he be the only one to get rich? Thor said. "We can lift it. I've always wanted to do something like a bank heist."

"You think you have the brain for that, stupid?"

Thor glared at him. "That big mouth of yours is going to get you in real trouble one day"

"I've been making it pretty good 'til now."

Thor punched his arm. "Let's get out of here before he comes back."

"We're not leaving those drugs behind, are we?" Eddie said.

"Hell, no."

Chapter 15

Thursday, Noon

Gina had crawled back into bed and slept until noon. She couldn't believe the time when she finally opened her eyes and sat up. She grabbed for her phone, remembering she'd turned it off in the middle of the night when she slipped out to see Vinnie. She'd meant to turn it on again, but forgot.

Harry had called three times.

She tapped his number. He picked up on the fourth ring.

"Hey, not like you to turn off your phone. What are you doing?"

"I'm just lazing around in bed. I stayed up too late and slept in."

At least that's not a lie.

"Listen, about last night … I didn't mean to sit on you. I'm just worried about you, doll. You're my person, I've got to take care of you."

"I know, but it gets suffocating sometimes, Harry. I'm not a delicate flower☐"

"Oh, Gina, you're pregnant! Let me baby you."

"No way! Remember, I'm from the Bronx. We're self-sufficient and tough. And that's the way I like it."

"Well, how's the warrior holding up?"

"Eh, I'll live. And are they working you to death?"

"Not at all. The census is down, so I guess there aren't enough patients to justify the extra staff. Administration asked me if I wanted to leave the assignment early … voluntarily, of course. You can bet your last dollar I snapped up that invitation."

"You're coming back?" Gina held her breath.

"I'll be home tomorrow."

"That's so cool," she lied again.

After they said their goodbyes, Gina collapsed back onto the bed. Every muscle was sore and aching from all the tension.

Oh, my god. What am I going to do? There's not enough time to grab Vinnie and get out of here before Harry gets home.

* * *

Peeking through the hole in the floor, the hermit watched the nurse talk on her cell phone. He liked her dark, curly hair and the way she talked. She looked up at the ceiling while her hands waved through the air. He could see from her eyes that she was unhappy and worried.

It made him feel strange. He wanted to pat her on the back to make her feel better. But he knew he couldn't do that. He had to be very careful. If anyone found out he was here, they might take him away, even kill him.

So many people have died here.

He'd almost been caught a few times when he couldn't seem to pay attention to what he was doing. It was dangerous when he left his floor and wandered through the building. He had to be extra, extra careful when he went down to the bottom floor and sneaked into the kitchen at night to bring back food to store. The bags were heavy and he knew he didn't dare drop one.

His attention returned to the hole in the floor.

There was something about the woman. He continued to stare at her. She seemed so tired, like she needed help. She made him feel like he had to take care of her and her baby.

* * *

"Did you find Vinnie?" Helen said the second Gina answered her phone. "I've been so worried about him ... and you."

She could hear the tremor in Helen's voice ... scared to death.

"Yes, I found him. He's drugged out and run down." Gina spoke very softly, like trying to calm a frightened child. "But he's okay, Helen."

"What's happening with you, though? You know you shouldn't be doing this."

"Oh, stop it already, Helen. I'm so up to my neck with everyone worrying about me. Harry's driving me nuts. Now that I'm about to be a mother, he wants to put me in a greenhouse and water me every day."

"The guy loves you. You're lucky."

"Yeah? What I am is totally screwed. Harry's coming home tomorrow and I don't know if I can find out what happened to Guy by then."

"Can *you* talk Vinnie into leaving with you?"

"If I can find out what happened to Guy, then he'll leave."

"Shoot, Gina. You don't know crap about that place. It's not like working here Ridgewood Hospital, where you know where everything is, how it all works."

"I'm going to do what I have to do to get my brother out of this hell hole." She barked out a laugh. "And for god's sake, don't you dare tell me to take care of myself."

* * *

Gina had to get her luggage from the Fiat. She was starting to go out the front door with a newspaper held over her head when Ziggy came out of her office.

"Here! Take this umbrella. It's pouring out there."

"You think it'll ever stop?"

"I honestly don't. You sure you want to go out there now?" There seemed to be a warning hidden in Ziggy's words."

"I'm feeling grubby enough that a little rain might be refreshing," she said with a smile. "Thanks so much for the 'brella."

She was about to leave when Ziggy gently took her arm. With a quick glance at Gina's belly, she said, "Be careful."

Gina could tell the receptionist wanted to say more. "I will be. I always try to be."

"No! You don't understand." All at once Ziggy looked like she was going to cry. "I don't want to see you get hurt." She squeezed Gina's arm. "If you need anything, let me know."

"Thanks, Ziggy."

Gina walked toward the car under the cover of Ziggy's umbrella. It was still pouring and she felt wet all over even with her head covered. There were about a dozen cars in the open carport and her Fiat looked as though it was smiling a hello. Just seeing it made her feel better. Vinnie's motorcycle was there, too.

She moved to the back of the car and started to open the trunk; she was startled by a shuffling noise. Thor stepped out from the back of the carport.

"Well, well! Lookee who's here." The orderly smiled at her, took an extra long drag on his cigarette, and made several perfectly round rings before blowing a long streaming trail of smoke at her. "Are you here for me, baby?"

"Not hardly!" She closed the umbrella and opened the trunk.

In a blur of motion, Thor flipped his cigarette and stepped up to the rear of the car. "Here, let me get that for you." He lifted the small piece of luggage out before she could say a word.

"That wasn't necessary□"

"Yeah, it was."

He slammed the trunk down, tossed the suitcase aside, and grabbed her around the waist. A hand rode over her breasts and belly.

"Get lost, you miserable creep!" She tried to twist away.

"Ya think that's gonna work for you, bitch?"

He shoved her hard against the trunk. His hands were fast as he tore open his scrub pants. "Think you're such hot shit … something special … special enough to get away from me."

Gina punched him square in the eye.

He just laughed. "A dingbat, knocked-up woman ain't getting away with that shit."

"Asshole!"

He snorted, "You don't stand a fucking chance in hell."

Gina pounded on his shoulders. It was like hitting a bunch of rocks.

"Let me go! Let me go!"

"Where I come from, we eat women like you for breakfast. Stuck-up bitch!"

He loosened his grip to pull at her scrubs. She shoved hard at his chest, kneed him in the balls. He fell to the ground.

"Son of a bitch!" He grit his teeth, clutched hard at his crotch.

Gina kicked him onto his back, grabbed the umbrella and jammed the point hard into his gut. He screamed out, tried to yank it away from her, but she snatched it and her suitcase and ran as hard as she could back to the entrance.

Inside, she hurried to Ziggy's office.

She dropped the suitcase and umbrella, bent over to try to catch her breath. Her soaked clothes dripped and slopped onto the tiled floor.

Ziggy reached out for her, led her to a chair. "What happened?"

When Gina could speak, she said, "I just slipped. Nothing serious."

When she looked up at Ziggy, she knew the woman didn't believe a word.

Chapter 16

Gina rolled her luggage into the elevator. She knew Ziggy was watching from her office; she could feel the woman's eyes boring through the back of her skull. She kept her chin high and nodded to Ziggy as she turned.

The door closed.

Then she collapsed, leaning heavily against the scarred back wall. She watched rainwater drip from her hair, jacket, and scrubs onto the dirty floor.

Exhaustion was pulling at every part of her body.

As the elevator climbed, she thought about what had happened with Thor. She hugged herself to stop from shaking.

Gina kept seeing it in her head. The memory rolled through her mind along with the horrible scenes that climbed up from the depths of her childhood.

Stop it!

But it was too late. Trauma always released a flash of herself as a scared Bronx teenager. Nothing held it back. Old memories piled one atop another and were ready to crush her.

Coming back from a movie, feeling happy, half-skipping on a quiet street. Alone. Totally alone.

Why did she have to go? She knew it wasn't safe to go without a friend so late in the day.

It was dusk and she knew she ought to hurry along. Walking the streets at night was stupid. But she was still caught up in the fantasy of the movie she'd just seen. A musical ... so happy, so beautiful. She did some dance steps, singing the songs to herself.

Smack!

A hand slammed against her mouth, another squeezed her neck, choking her until she couldn't breathe.

85

Helpless. She was totally helpless. She couldn't see his face but he was strong, dragging her into a nearby alley. No one answered her screams when he threw her to the ground, straddled her legs, and struggled to strip down her jeans.

She punched his face over and over, a face she never forgot, one that still waits for her in all of her nightmares.

She freed a leg, kicked hard at that face, again and again. When he let go, she ran.

Yes, she'd gotten away, but she'd always hated herself for running. Even if it was the only way she could have escaped then … and today.

It had almost happened again. And being raped would certainly end her pregnancy.

Gina's fist curled into a tight ball.

One day, I promise I will stand, I will not run and I will beat these bullies down so they can feel what it's like to be cornered and humiliated.

* * *

Delores hurried down the hall as Gina was about to walk into her room.

"Glad I caught you."

Gina wanted to shove her luggage into the room and slam the door in Delores's face. She needed to strip out of her wet clothes and tumble into a shower. Instead, she turned and smiled at the supervisor. "I have to get out of these sopping things pretty quick."

"Good. I see you got your luggage." She'd barely finished the sentence when she added, "Is there any chance we can change your hours today to the night shift?"

Gina hesitated before answering. "Not my favorite hours to work … but sure."

Delores Smiley finally lived up to her name and gave Gina a huge smile. "The night nurse is sick. Her whole family's down with the flu."

"Okay," Gina said. "I'm sorry, but I've got to get into my room and change."

"Yes, you are kind of wet. Well, thanks for helping out." Delores turned and walked down the hall.

Gina hurried inside, locked the door, put the chair under the door knob, and pulled her clothes off. She was under the warm shower in less than a minute. She could feel sore spots everywhere from her battle with Thor. She took an inventory of her body and was pretty sure nothing terrible had happened that would affect her pregnancy. She'd been very lucky … this time.

* * *

Donnie, the hermit, watched the woman squirm out of her clothes. He noticed again that she was pregnant. He watched in awe as she ran both hands across her round tummy. He had a vague remembrance of his mother doing the same thing when she was carrying his little brother. It made him feel calm.

After a while she tossed the wet clothes she'd been wearing onto the floor before stepping into the bathroom. When she came out, she pulled fresh clothes from her suitcase.

Seeing her made him sad.

He wanted to go home, wanted to see his mother again, but he couldn't remember where she was. How would he find her when they took away all his memories in that room on the bottom floor?

Every night after he stole his food he would sneak down to that room to see if he could find his memories waiting. But inside, even when he touched all the things in the room, all he felt was confusion. No matter how hard he tried, everything remained a near blank.

He turned away from his viewing hole and lugged himself down the hall, back to his corner. Once there, he flashed the walls with a Maglite he'd stolen. All the pictures on the wall were from old magazines he'd found lying around; they glowed with the light. He rubbed his fingers over them and smiled. He was sure the women looked like his mom even though all the people he once knew, even his mother, were only blurry pictures in his mind.

* * *

Gina tapped Harry's cell number. She couldn't go another moment without hearing his voice. She pulled at her short tufts of hair to make the time hurry along, but it seemed to take forever.

"Hi, babe."

Damn hormones. She felt like she was going to burst into tears. "Oh, Harry, I miss you so much."

"Hey, are you all right? You sound like you've been crying."

"Oh, no, just feeling blue and a little sentimental ... and missing you."

"Well, I'll be home tomorrow. Tell you what, I'll drag out the Scrabble set and beat your pants off." He laughed. "You'll wish I hadn't come home."

"That's never going to happen."

"What's never going to happen?"

"Either one." She swiped at tears streaming down her cheeks. "You're not going to win ... and I'll never stop missing you when you're away."

* * *

Vinnie lined up at the nurses' station window. It was time to take his meds. He needed to keep his head straight and the more meds he took the less he was he able to concentrate. The pills not only wore him down, but within a half hour after swallowing them he became listless and unfocused.

Standing before the station window, he and the nurse, Lena, glared at each other.

"Thinking about another stretch tied down to a gurney, fella?"

He shook his head and picked up the small, paper cup holding his meds. Lena eyed his every move.

"Water?" she asked.

"Nope. They slide down easily enough."

"Take the water." This time it wasn't a request. He took a swallow and handed the cup back to her.

"Finish it, soldier."

He drained the cup and set it down.

"Open your mouth and lift your tongue."

When she finished inspecting the inside of his mouth, she said, "I think you're getting the hang of it."

Vinnie walked down the hall, knew it wouldn't be too many minutes before he wouldn't care too much about anything.

In his room, Dallas was sprawled across his bed reading a magazine.

"Come on, Dallas. I need to find a way to get out of taking these drugs. I need your help, man."

"What's the difference? It's a helluva way to kill time, especially when nothing hurts.

Vinnie knew their other roommate, Rick Bell, was far behind him in the med line and it would be a little while before he came back. He sat on the side of his own bed facing Dallas.

"The only reason I'm in this shithole is because my friend died here a few weeks back."

Dallas kept reading his magazine. "Yeah, so?"

"Come on. The dude was my best buddy in Afghanistan."

Dallas tossed the magazine onto the floor. "Do you really think I give a rat's ass?"

"I think you do," Vinnie said. "I need your help."

"So what is it you think I can do for you?"

Vinnie's head was starting to spin. "I need to stop taking these medications so I can snoop around and find out what happened to Guy West."

Dallas sat up. "Guy West was your buddy?"

"Yeah. I told you before. You didn't seem interested."

Dallas nodded to the empty bed against the wall. "That was his bed before he died."

Vinnie had to lie down. His mind was starting to drift away and he barely heard what Dallas said.

"Sleep it off, buddy." Dallas patted his arm. "We'll talk later."

Chapter 17

Thursday, Late Afternoon-Early Evening

Delores sat across from Norman in his office; it wasn't much bigger than hers. She stared hard at his pasty face and noticed that he was looking very tired and was acting more dour these days. When they first started working together, he at least had a dry sense of humor. But that one saving grace had definitely disappeared.

It had been ten years and this was the third Veterans Affairs hospital they would be closing. She remembered how they were first hired by officials of the VA to systematically improve low-performing hospitals. That was a laugh. Both were taken out of service by the two of them. "Improvement" was just a euphemism for shutting them down.

"So, Delores," he said, interrupting her thoughts, "we're quickly approaching the end of the road."

She nodded, continued to stare at him. Finally, she said, "Everything seems to be going as planned." She shifted in her hardback chair. "Have you told Manky the news?"

"Not yet."

"I'm glad you're the one who has to deal with him." Just thinking about it made her angry. "I didn't get involved with this to deal with a Manky Olav."

"Well, I don't like it either … but money's money, and he's been the perfect middleman."

"Until you cross him or do something he doesn't like."

"Well, Ms. Smiley, just remember, you're into this as deep as I am. He won't push only me to the wall."

"Look, Norman, I've been thinking about this for a while." Delores leaned forward. "I want out. I can't do this anymore. You can keep the money. I just want to go back to being a nurse again."

He stared at her for a long moment and then broke out laughing until tears ran down his cheeks.

"You want out? Listen, wanna-be-a-nurse-again. That time has long passed. You don't get to make decisions like that anymore. You're up to your neck in this and there's no turning back."

* * *

After taking his medication, Rick Bell hit the sack, stretched out, and slid out the vodka bottle from under the bed. He slugged down huge gulps of the clear liquor, barely feeling the burn as it hit his stomach.

He thanked his lucky stars that booze wasn't that hard to get, because the pills alone didn't do squat for him. He still heard the screams of men dying and their voices clung to him like moss on a tree.

Besides, he had nothing else to do with his money, so bribing Eddie to slip the liquor into the hospital wasn't much of a hardship. That dude would do anything for a buck.

Man, he'd rather deal with Eddie than Thor. That fool had no heart; he'd beat you just for the hell of it. And he had. Many times.

Rick's eyes were drooping and he chuckled to himself as he remembered the night he and his buddies got high and decided to enlist in the army.

The party they hosted turned out to be a real bash. Rick thought that by morning all the drug-induced bravery would vanish like a fart in the breeze.

But it didn't.

The five of them had no real prospects for jobs and didn't know what they wanted to do with the rest of their lives. Three of the five were deployed to Afghanistan in the same unit.

He was the lone survivor.

After a year, they tossed his ass out with a medical discharge. Yeah, he'd lost a leg when an IED blew it off, but he thought he'd gotten by that until the nightmares and panic attacks began sucking up all his energy. After he slashed two wrists to the bone, his private doc got him into Bone Point … the only place that would take him in.

When he had a sudden urge to barf, Rick turned to his side and stared at Dallas. But the feeling passed and he took some deep breaths. His head was spinning and his stomach still felt really weird. As he started to pass out, Eddie and Thor appeared out of nowhere, stood next to his bed.

"Did you add the Vicodin to the vodka bottle?" Thor asked.

"Do I look like a complete idiot to you?"

"Well, Eddie, now that you ask." Thor roared with laughter.

Rick was sluggish, thought about what they were saying.

Who are they talking about?

Did they spike my booze?

Although Rick couldn't open his eyes, he could hear every word the two men said.

He finally forced his lids open and stared into Dallas Dacy's hard, gray eyes. The man quickly turned away. Then Rick looked over at Vinnie. But he was sound asleep. Or was he passed out?

"Eddie, what's going on? Why do I feel so sick?"

"Hey, man," Eddie said. "It's just the booze. You drank too much."

"No! I want to get up. Help me get my leg on, get out of here. Come on."

"Oh, shut up, you loser," Thor said. His fist came down and pounded his face. Now all Rick felt was pain. He slid into a dark hole.

* * *

Eddie helped Thor lift Rick onto a gurney. They rode the elevator down to the Tunnel and brought him to a room where two other men were already passed out on beds.

Rick was now barely sucking in air. The two others they'd brought down weren't doing too much breathing either.

"Why did ya have to hit him? He was already out of it." Eddie was pissed at Thor. "I swear, you're the meanest critter I've ever met."

"Sheesh, did you think I wanted to hear him groan all the way down to this hole? He's gonna check out, that's all I care about."

Eddie looked over at the other two men. "Looks like they're all set to go. And I do mean go."

"Yeah, this gig's getting pretty dull," Thor said. "It was sort of fun at first. Now it's just damn boring."

"They should've died fighting over there. Shouldn't have to go through all this shit," Eddie said. "I guess maybe we're really doing these vets a favor."

"Yeah, yeah. Whatever floats your boat, loser." Thor reached out a hand. "Pass me the pillow. I ain't gonna spend the whole night getting this done."

The two of them stood on either side of the bed and positioned the pillow over Rick Bell's face. In unison, they pressed down hard and held tight over his struggle to breathe before they moved onto the others.

Chapter 18

Dallas Dacy's insides were churning. He'd looked hard at the two orderlies when they flung Rick Bell around like a bundle of dirty laundry, tossed him onto a gurney, and wheeled him out of the room.

They'd both avoided looking directly at Dallas. His "hands off" status had held him in good stead for two years. But it was getting harder and harder to keep his mouth zipped when his fellow vets were getting beat up, particularly when they were passive, drugged out of their minds, and couldn't fight back.

Eddie and Thor? Fucking cowards.

But Dallas did what he was told by Norman and Delores, did their dirty work and kept his nose out of everyone's business. It was no skin off his ass what happened to anyone else. He got what he needed: room and board and a small piece of change. It was a pretty good free ride. Anything was better than living on the streets.

But it's getting harder to turn away.

He didn't like what Eddie and Thor had done to Guy West. And now he knew what they were going to do to Rick Bell.

Yeah, he knew about the orderlies and their end of the equation. It didn't mean he had to like it. And these days he was liking it less and less.

Vinnie Mazzio was stupid to put himself into this hell hole for Guy. The man was gone and that was that.

Dallas had liked Guy even though he knew how really sick he was. Like so many others, he was a good man who gave up everything for his country and ended up being nothing but a slab of cold meat.

Dallas had taken a few bad whops trying to keep Guy from crushing his own skull. Guy would get up in the middle of the night and start banging his head against the wall. Guy never remembered much about his nightmares; all he talked about were the loud noises in his head.

Dallas knew about those explosions. Just about anybody in this place knew about them. After three deployments, first to Iraq, the last two to Afghanistan, Dallas heard screaming men and bombs blasting his brain most nights, too. He'd learned to put up with it. The trick was learning what was real and what wasn't.

But right up to the end, when Dallas finished a tour, he came back ready to sign up again. He needed the money to keep his sister in college; his mom and dad couldn't swing it. But the last time he failed the psych check.

The Army dumped him.

All those years I put in. They squeezed all the juice out of me and in the end they just dumped me like toxic waste. Used me up and burned me out.

Goodbye. Oh, and by the way, thanks for your fucking service.

When he came back, he couldn't face his family.

Dallas left behind his namesake, Dallas, Texas, the only place he'd ever wanted to live.

He drifted from city to city. He ended up in San Francisco, wandering around for weeks, sleeping on shit-filled sidewalks until he found a small isolated alley where he paid a bottle of booze to take over a refrigerator box. After that, every day he fought hard to hang on to that spot.

One night, he lost it in a knife fight.

Dallas didn't know exactly how Norman Glick found him. Maybe it was the doc at the free street clinic where he was treated for the slash he got during the struggle for the box.

"You're going to have to come back regularly so we can take care of this," she said.

"No way!"

96

The doc looked at him with soft eyes, but her back was rigid and her words were harsh.

"You either come back or you're going to lose that arm for sure. Not only that, it'll probably kill you."

"It doesn't look that bad."

She smiled at him. "Really? Then why are you here?"

The booze he'd slugged down earlier was wearing off. He didn't want to see the doc again. He just wanted to be left alone.

"I can't make you come here. It's up to you."

Maybe I'd be better off dead. This isn't much of a life.

But he knew he wasn't ready to die. He wanted to see his mother and father again. Beg his sister's forgiveness for running out on her.

He came back every day for ten days for a dressing change and medication. On his final day, this guy in a suit walked up to him.

"How'd you like to come work for me?"

Dallas eyed him, said, "Doing what?"

"What do you care?" He took a business card from his pocket and handed it to Dallas.

Norman Glick
Administrator
Bone Point Veterans Hospital

Still not sure if he wanted any job, he said, "I'm not exactly dressed to work anywhere."

"If you want the work, we'll get you some clothes and drive you to the hospital today. It's about sixty miles north on the coast."

The man waited patiently for his decision.

Finally Dallas held out his hand. "My name is Dallas Dacy."

It had been two years since he took the job. In the first year he was in a kind of daze, just happy to have a roof over his head. But now he was starting to wake up.

Chapter 19

Gina had crawled back into bed, snuggled into the blanket. and fell into a deep sleep. She'd slept the rest of the day away. When she finally awakened, she barely had time to put on fresh clothes and fly down the stairs to make it to the nurses' station on time for the night shift.

She was breathless when she unlocked the station door. She was surprised to find Lena, obviously anxious to leave.

"I was beginning to have my doubts about your getting here," Lena said.

"Oh, no. No reason to come early … you'd only put me to work." She looked at Lena's solemn face. "Hey, I'm just messing with you."

Lena seemed to relax.

"I thought you worked the day shift, Lena."

"Delores did some shuffling to get coverage. The swing shift RN is still out sick." Lena gave her a fleeting smile and stood. "Nothing unusual going on. This will probably be very boring. A long stretch of time to get through. Too bad you didn't bring anything to read."

"I didn't think about it."

"Well, if you get desperate, there're some really, really outdated magazines in that bottom drawer." She pointed to it as she reached for the door. "By the way, the on-call night tech is in the back room if you need her. Her name's Amy. She's a great kid."

"Okay."

After Lena left, Gina sat at the computer and went through the patient files. Three names were marked for discharge in the am shift. Two of the names she didn't recognize, but she knew Rick

Bell was one of Vinnie's roommates. All three had a "D" next to their names.

She tapped her fingers on the desk for several moments before she pulled a Maglite from a drawer, stepped out into the corridor, which had very little lighting. She locked the station door behind her. Her flashlight stabbed through the darkness, projecting an eerie, bobbing ray of light as she walked down the hall. The walls seemed to close in with dark shadows that reached out for her.

At Vinnie's room she tried to open the door quietly but it gave a small squeak. She shined the light on Vinnie. He was snoring loudly and was really out of it.

Then she looked over at Rick Bell's bed.

What happened? Where is he? Why is his bed torn up, his sheets scattered every which way? He's supposed to be discharged in the morning.

When she flashed onto Dallas's bed, the man stared back with eyes that glowed.

"Where's Rick?"

"Gone."

"Everything all right, Dallas? Anything you want to tell me?"

He smiled at her. "I drew the short stick. I have night duty."

She hesitated, then smiled back at him. "Me, too."

* * *

Friday, 2:00 am

It was 2:00 am before Gina felt safe enough to leave the station again. She had her switchblade in her pocket and the long hours of sleep had revived her enough that she almost felt like her normal self.

Whatever that is.

She knocked at the on-call room.

"Yeah?"

100

"Amy, I left something in my room," Gina said. "Could you go to the station ... cover for me while I'm gone? I'll be back soon."

"No problem." She was up and out heading for the station in an instant.

Gina wasn't about to get caught in the decrepit elevator. She slid her pass card through the stairway door security slot and hurried down the one flight to the first floor. She checked out the corridor. It was empty.

Gina had already met the night shift security guard and decided a feather would easily knock him over. But she knew he was somewhere in the building prowling around.

Or maybe sleeping in a corner.

Finally, standing in front of Delores's office, she carefully turned the doorknob. It opened silently; she slipped inside the dimly lit room and headed straight for the file cabinet. She was about to flip on her Maglite when the glass door lit up.

Damn it! Security!

Gina lay down on the floor behind the desk, stuck her feet in the knee hole, and wiggled in until most of her was under the desk. With her baby bump, it was a tight and awkward fit.

She heard the door open.

Fear, claustrophobia immediately kicked in. Hyperventilating, she knew in another minute she'd be out cold.

A light bounced around for a couple of seconds before the door closed.

Almost paralyzed, she eased back and tried to lift herself up, but her belly screamed in pain. She squashed her panic by pushing to stretch out, but there wasn't enough room. She kept her eyes closed until the spasm faded.

This is what lying around doing nothing does to you.

She opened her eyes and saw a sheet of paper sitting on her belly. Pieces of tape protruded from all four sides. It must have been affixed to the underside of the desk. She grabbed it, turned on her flashlight, and saw it held several lines of numbers. Two were crossed out in pencil, leaving three that were unmarked.

Passwords?

Gina pushed back until she was entirely clear of the knee-hole and was pressed up against the desk chair. Twisting around, she grabbed the seat of the chair and pushed herself up onto her knees. By the time she was fully standing, she was covered in sweat that dotted her scrubs. She felt like she'd battled a bear.

Delores's computer seemed to stare at her, daring her to try the numbers.

She sat down at the desk, looked at the blinking cursor for a moment. She tapped in the first available line of numbers, which must have been chosen at random; there was no discernible pattern.

She chuckled to herself.

Just like new math.

The numbers she'd tapped in were worthless. She was locked out.

She moved onto the second line. She was still blocked.

Sweat bubbled on her forehead as she got ready for the last line of numbers. Would some kind of security alarm go off on the third try if this line of digits wasn't the pass code?

Her finger hovered over the enter key. As she pressed down, she closed her eyes and then opened them.

She was in!

She carefully re-taped the list of numbers back under the desktop before opening the files.

She wasn't sure what she was looking for, but she tapped into discharges and tried to single out the ones who'd died.

What stood out the most was that hundreds of vets were still listed as in-house patients. And yet she knew there were actually only fifteen patients left at Bone Point.

Scores of names had the letter "D" next to their listing.

"D" for discharge? "D" for double listed? "D" for dead?

Rick Bell had a "D" next to his name.

What were they up to?

Why were there so many people still listed as inpatients?

She closed her eyes. All at once she knew.

Oh, my god. The duplicitous bastards are ghosting people. Claiming they are alive when they're dead.

Her eye started to twitch again. She knew she was taking too much time.

Need to get back to the unit.

Closing down the computer, she eyed the file cabinet. Ignoring her intuition to leave right away, she walked over to it. She was surprised there was no lock. But then, who would want to try to mess with Delores's files?

Except me.

Inside the top drawer were mostly employee records that dated back three years. There were a few other administrative business files that didn't interest Gina. And believe it or not, a file for food recipes. Now she knew why there was no need for a lock. There was nothing here that was going to give Gina anything important.

A chill ran down her spine. She needed to get out. Now!

She stopped to listen for the security guard.

Silence.

Before leaving, she quickly opened the second file drawer. There was only one folder, and it had no labeling or designation. All that was inside was a list of different delivery dates.

Delivery of what?

The dates were spaced weekly. One delivery was due tomorrow. She looked at her watch. Or rather, today.

She checked the hallway before going back up to the patient floor.

* * *

It was four in the morning. Gina's mind was in high gear, but she was still trapped in the nurses station in the middle of her shift.

Whatever made Vinnie think something unusual happened to Guy West was beginning to resonate. Gina now had her own questions.

His counselor, Pablo, said Guy was really in a bad place.

So did Vinnie.

Although her brother could be a real hothead, this didn't feel like he'd jumped into something blindly. He wouldn't walk out on Helen unless he was onto something serious.

She brought Rick Bell's file up on the computer in the nurses' station. He was still listed as an in-house patient with the letter "D" next to his name.

This was like Delores's computer file.

Gina tried to dig through all the recent deaths at Bone Point,

The computer wouldn't give her the information. She was only able to go back one month. But ten veterans had a "D" listed next to their names in the last month, including Guy West and Rick Bell. There were few death certificates but they all gave the same cause of death hypoxia. Pathologist's note: Probably cause: medications mixed with alcohol.

Pathologist's note?

Gina could find no evidence of an autopsy ever being performed on anyone.

Chapter 20

Gina knew that Vinnie's roommate, Rick Bell, was alive yesterday. And he was taken from his room during the swing shift or else the messed-up sheets would have been long gone.

Where did they take him? Why?

Gina paced back and forth in the nurses' station, amazed at how vitalized she felt. And then it happened. She stopped dead in her tracks.

The baby kicked .

OMG!

It's really alive. Not just a ghostly image in a sono.

Our baby is real!

She snapped her cell phone from her pocket and tapped Harry's cell. It rang four times before he picked up.

"Gina, are you all right?" His voice was sleepy and worried.

She could barely speak. "Our ... baby..."

"What is it?"

"It just kicked me. It's really alive, Harry!"

A loud howl into the phone made her laugh.

"Oh, babe ... I'm so glad you called."

"Me, too."

"That's the best news ever. I'll see you tomorrow. I can't wait."

* * *

This would be her last chance to wander through the Tunnel when no one else was around. Because, hell or high water, she was getting out of here later today, and so was Vinnie.

She needed to get to that bottom floor and look around.

It was strange. Whenever anyone mentioned the Tunnel, their voices changed. Even Delores Smiley seemed to gulp a few times after she mentioned it.

Something was definitely off about that floor.

Also, it was pretty strange for a live patient to be discharged in the next shift but still not be available. Was Rick Bell dead?

The morgue was in the Tunnel and Rick Bell, if he was dead, should be there waiting for a funeral home to pick him up. She had to see for herself.

Gina stepped out into the corridor from the nurses' station and stood listening for a long moment before she felt it was safe to proceed. Hurrying along, she did a fast sweep of the patient rooms to make sure everyone was all right. Everything and everyone was quiet. Even Dallas was asleep when she peeked into Vinnie's room.

She awakened the on-call nursing tech again. She'd gone back to sleep in the spare room, dressed in her scrubs.

"Hey, sorry to wake you, Amy, but I have an upset stomach. I'll probably be in the john for a while. I don't want to have to worry about the patients while I'm gone."

"Are any of them having problems?"

Only in the head.

"No, they're all asleep."

"Okay." Amy turned and got comfortable, ready to go back to sleep.

"Hey, Amy! Up and at 'em. You need to go to the nurses station and stay there until I get back." She gave the tech her cell number. "If you need me right away, just call."

Amy gave Gina an angry glare, but she got out of bed and headed down the corridor to the nurses' station.

Gina took to the stairs again and walked down to the bottom floor. She stuck her head out and listened until she was convinced no one was around. The lights in the corridor were brighter here and she could actually see in both directions.

She turned to the right and soon she peeked into the ECT room: restraints for the wrists and ankles were attached to a table. Dimmed night lights displayed a clean area loaded with the expected equipment: EKG, ECT monitors, Oxygen tank, and other odds and ends needed for the procedure.

Staring into the silent room without the drama of a patient undergoing his brain being forced into a seizure, or the staff working   starting IVs, bagging the patient with oxygen, or the general flurry of activity, it didn't seem like such a big deal. But the reality was so much bigger.

How depressed do you have to be before someone fries your brain?

Gina felt a shiver crawl up and down her spine.

* * *

The hermit woke up with a start. It was time to get up. Very early morning was Donnie's favorite part of the day. He could walk freely up and down the corridors, snooping around for loose magazines and things that might be left around that were interesting. He liked to pretend he still had the freedom to come and go, but he knew that wasn't true. He couldn't be discovered. If he was, he'd be locked up forever.

Sometimes he thought about leaving. He could walk out the door; no one knew he was here, except Ziggy. But he didn't know where he would go if he wasn't here. This had become his home.

He walked through the shadows into one of the old, deserted patient bathrooms. There, he washed his face and beard, washed under his arms. When he was dry, he used one of the deodorants he'd found discarded. He liked the aroma.

Studying himself in the mirror, he knew he wasn't old, only twenty-five, but his beard was completely white, while the hair on his head was still black as coal, like his eyes.

He'd slept most of the previous day and now he was very hungry. His supply of food was very low.

Using a security pass he'd stolen, he quietly made his way to the Tunnel, and was in the kitchen, gathering up food supplies when he heard someone open the staircase door. He hid in a corner behind the refrigerator and peeked out to see who was out and around besides him.

He saw the new nurse pass by the door. What was *she* doing here at this hour?

* * *

Gina turned around and walked to the other end of the hallway. There were two doors that probably led to storage rooms. They were locked down with numbered security pads to keep people out who didn't have authorization to enter.

She thought about it for a moment, then shrugged and moved on to the next room.

Gina flipped on the light; there were three beds. Next to each one, pillows and blankets were stacked on a chair. Even from the doorway, she could tell they were clean. She sniffed the air.

This room was used recently. For what?

She turned away and stopped at the next door, marked with a sign:

MORGUE

She opened the door and stepped into the chilled room. There were three bodies lying on wooden tables.

OMG! What am I doing here?

She patted her belly and said, "Hey, little one. This is nothing unusual. Don't be scared. This is just something mommy does every now and then. No one is going to hurt you."

She walked up to the nearest table and pulled down the sheet at the head

It was someone she hadn't met in the short time she'd been at Bone Point. The same for the next table.

The last one held the body of Rick Bell.

Chapter 21

Gina looked down at the dead vet. Rick had been alive this very night, right before she came on duty. And now he was dead.

It made her think of all the others who died before him.

Tears trickled down her cheek. She swiped them away.

All those men and women are ordered into battle to kill or be killed, while at home we continue on with our everyday lives. Do we give a second thought about how they suffer while we shop for clothes, watch our action movies, laugh at the television. Yes, we occasionally read about it, hear about it in the news. But does it really get to us? Do we ever care enough?

She ran a finger across Rick's cheek. Cold. Lifeless.

I'm so sorry, Rick.

She turned to leave, her thoughts lost in her own brother and how his PTSD affected his life and everyone who loved him. When he came back from Afghanistan he wasn't the little brother that went away. He was☐

"Ouch!"

Someone had grabbed her arm, spun her around.

"Hey!" she yelled out.

Gina stared into Thor's cruel eyes. Eddie was standing next to him, a nasty smirk on his face

Her heart raced, her whole body was throbbing. She could barely catch her breath.

"So the little nurse likes to snoop," Thor said.

"Let go of my arm!" Gina tried to pull back from him.

He yanked her arm so hard she screamed. Pain jolted through her shoulder.

Eddie was laughing now.

"Let's get this bitch into ECT," Thor said.

"No!"

She fought hard, punched at him with her free arm. But she couldn't stop him from dragging her down the hall.

Eddie yelled, "Yahoo! There'll be a hot time in the old town tonight."

At the doorway to the ECT room, Thor pulled her up tight against him, ran his hand up and down her body, forced his fist between her legs. "See that table ... see those restraints? That's where you're going. We're gonna lay you down and give that baby of yours some real company."

"Stop it! Leave me alone!"

"You don't get to kick *me* in the balls, bitch."

"Let me go, you idiot. I'm pregnant. I could lose my baby."

"Do you think I give a royal□"

Everything suddenly went dark. Gina blinked, trying to see through the inky blackness, but there was nothing but the sound of a heavy thud.

Eddie must have fallen down. He yelled, "Hey! Man, that hurt!"

Gina kicked Thor, blindly punched him. He let go. Someone else was punching him, too. Thor bounced hard against her before sliding down.

A man's harsh whisper blasted in her ear. "Come with me, lady. Now!"

Whoever it was, grabbed her hand. Together they ran down the corridor until they were at the dimly lit staircase. It happened so fast all she caught was the flash of a white beard.

"Run!"

Then he was gone, swallowed up in the darkness of the corridor.

She raced up the stairs. Back on the second floor, she took a moment to lean over, rest her hands on her thighs. She was shivering.

Like this morning, she could have been raped. Could have lost her baby.

The nursing tech came towards her. "You've been gone for an hour. Where have you been?"

"Were there any problems? You never called," Gina said, finally catching her breath.

"Well, what took you so long?"

"I'm sorry if I worried you," Gina said, avoiding answering the question. She touched Amy's shoulder. "Thanks for covering for me. I really appreciate it."

Amy gave her a shy smile. "Oh, it's all right."

"Go and grab some more shut-eye if you can."

Gina watched the nursing tech take off down the hall. When she was out of sight, Gina unlocked the nurses' station, bolted it behind her and collapsed into a chair.

* * *

"Who the hell was that," Thor spat out to Eddie.

"Was it one of the vets?" Eddie was rubbing his side. "Damn, I'm gonna have a helluva bruise."

Thor was pretty shaken himself, from having fallen down so hard.

"It can't be any of the vets," Thor said. "They're so zoned out, they'd fall down before we did … that is if they could even make it to the Tunnel."

Thor was bummed. Feeling mean.

"Did you get to see what he looked like?" Eddie asked.

"Sometimes you mouth the stupidest questions." Thor wanted to punch him, really mess him up. "How the hell was I gonna see anyone? It was pitch black."

"I guess," Eddie said.

"That nurse is gonna get it. Get it good."

Thor knew he sounded really angry that the nurse got away, but what he really wanted to do was cry.

She shouldn't have run away. Left me like that.

Whenever anything went wrong in his life, those same words would race through his head.

She shouldn't have run away. Left me like that.

He was only eight when his mother dumped him at the doorstep of a Catholic church. He remembered that he couldn't stop crying. The nuns placed him in one of their orphanages and they kept him there until he ran away just before he turned eighteen.

Yeah, I'd had enough of them.

They'd been okay but he was finished; all they wanted him to do was read books. He didn't want to spend his time being around those prissy nuns one more day. His mother had been beautiful, the nuns were old and fat. Even the young ones had pimply faces with thin lips.

Thor knew Eddie's story, and it was pretty much the same, only he went from foster home to foster home until he ran away, too.

They'd met at a party one night, both drunk out of their minds, and started hanging out together. He liked Eddie, but he still was a dumb boob.

The two of them were the last orderlies left who had worked at Bone Point for any length of time. Now all the others were temps who floated in and out of the hospital.

Bet that costs them a pretty penny.

Eddie interrupted his thoughts. "What do you think is really in those locked up closets that Norman was into?"

"Give it a minute, will you." Thor glared at him. "We get beaten up and the nurse is snatched and that's all you can think of?" Thor looked away in disgust. "You really are an idiot."

* * *

Gina, back in the nurses station, heard them coming down the corridor. They weren't even trying to sneak up on her. It was if they wanted her to know what she was up against.

One of them kicked at the nurses' station door and rattled the doorknob.

"Come out, come out wherever you are," Thor sang in a sing-song way.

"Get lost, you loser," Gina said on the other side of the door.

He rattled the doorknob again. Harder.

Eddie said, "Come on. We didn't mean nothing. We were just playin' with you."

"You losers better get lost before I call security. Or the cops."

"You shouldn't have left us like that, all hurt and beat up."

"I would have kicked your faces in if I could have. Now get out of here!"

"Ooooooooh, she's really scary, isn't she? Come on, Eddie. Let's leave the bitch alone."

She heard them talk as they moved away from the door.

Man, oh man. I have to grab Vinnie and get away from here.

Chapter 22

Friday, 5:00 am

Manky Olav was a light sleeper. He was jumpy even with three of his most trusted men standing guard right outside his door.

The bedside clock assaulted him with its garish, orange 5:01.

He should have felt secure in his elegant country home surrounded by two super alert German shepherds roaming the grounds, along with his AR-15-equipped bodyguards. They were ready for anything.

But Manky didn't inherit his mob status only by DNA alone, or just trusting anyone.

He knew an invisible neon bull's-eye flashed on his back, day and night. That's what you can expect when you're a drug czar, the man in charge. His was an extra huge target for any one of his competitors to see and there were plenty of them. Other big honchos had tried to snatch or kill him several times over the years.

Even he was surprised he'd managed to live forty-two years.

If they could grab him, they would chop off his head. That was the quick ritual Manky used all the time when he was feeling generous. He could only hope it would be that fast and easy for him.

He knew better.

A beheading or a bullet to the head wasn't the type of exit he was ever going to get if his *compadres* cornered him.

He looked at the bedside clock again: 5:15.

Manky thought about his Grandpa Alexi.

He would always say, "Try to be a decent man, Manky. Try very hard. Only if you must, kill anyone who tries to move in on you. Decency is for those who do as they're told."

Manky smiled when he remembered his grandpa. When Manky was very little, his grandpa would bounce him on his knee and tell him stories about Russia and the old country. One day when Manky was ten, Grandpa was gone.

"What happened to Grandpa? Where is he?" Manky asked his Papa every single day.

One day, Papa said, "Don't ask about him again. He's gone."

"But, Papa, what□"

His father slapped him hard in the face. "I said that's enough."

There was no more talk about Grandpa Alexi. He just disappeared from his life. Later on, Manky had his suspicions, but he never knew for sure and he never asked again.

Passing time hadn't changed anything. He still thought about the happy memories of his Grandpa Alexi.

5:47 am.

When Manky was ten, right at the time his Grandpa Alexi disappeared, his father began teaching him about the business, made sure he learned how to rule their organization.

Manky remembered the first time his papa sat him down into a chair to watch something.

"I don't like this place, Papa."

They were in the basement, in a room Manky had never seen before. It was cold and it smelled funny. Not a good funny.

"This is how we deal with traitors, my son."

"Why is there a plastic sheet on the floor, Papa?"

"It's neater that way. You'll see."

Then his father's "friends" brought in a naked, screaming man. They tied the bloodied prisoner into a chair.

"Please, I didn't do it. I've been set up." The man's face was covered in tears that kept gushing from his eyes.

"So, Manky," his Papa said. "It was your grandpa who taught me how to do deal with traitors. He was very meticulous. He liked to start with the ears, then he wanted every single extremity

116

removed before he gouged out the eyes. You see, grandpa wanted the traitor to see, to experience everything right up to the end."

He nodded to the man standing over a table of cutting instruments that also had a small saw.

The screams were a crescendo that ended in high-pitched shrieks. It was unbearable. Manky remembered covering his own ears as he watched the man's ears being cut loose from his head.

Manky was crying and screaming like the man. At one point he covered his eyes, but his papa tore his hands away from his face.

"Look and learn."

Papa waited until the screams of innocence and sobs quieted. Then Papa nodded to the man and he scooped out the traitor's eyes. Without waiting, he cut out the man's tongue.

Manky ran from the room, vomited with every step out of there.

Over the years, Papa taught him this careful process. When Manky was around thirteen, it stopped bothering him and he began to pay attention.

Now, any time anyone tried to seize his power, or refused to do what he was told, Manky stopped trying to be a decent man the way his Grandpa Alexi taught him.

He turned and looked at his beside clock.

Fucking 5:50

He flipped onto his side and almost dosed off, but something kept nagging at him. Something was off. He rolled back and forth from one side of the bed to the other. Then back again,

Now, he was even more wide awake.

He swung his legs around and was up and robed in an instant. He walked from his bedroom to his office, his men trailing him. He sat down at his desk, pulled out his appointment book, and opened it.

In bold letters was the name Dallas Dacy. His "appointment" was for later today.

Chapter 23

The orderlies were in the Tunnel guzzling beer and planning how they were going to corner the pregnant nurse and beat the hell out of her.

"Both inside and out," Eddie said.

Thor laughed. He could go without sleep, stay up forever as long as he had a cool one in his hand. But when he drank, which was whenever he could, his mind always wandered back to his short time in the Army. How he beat up a female soldier … broke her leg.

Well, she deserved it. Don't back out of a fuck because you change your mind at the last minute. Not with me.

They tossed his ass with a dishonorable discharge … said he was lucky he didn't end up in the cooler. They call this life lucky?

Hell that was a long time ago.

He looked at Eddie through blurry eyes. The dude never seemed to be able to a have decent conversation. It was always sixth-grade sludge pouring out of his mouth.

Thor said, "Who the hell do you think that was who flipped the lights and sucker punched us?"

"Like I said before, one of the vets must have gotten loose, or somethin'."

Eddie looked pretty boozed up and they'd only had three or four beers. Thor wanted to mess him up but he needed the dude to check out the old security system. The whole thing had been shut down six months ago and Thor didn't know squat about how to fix it or start it up.

He watched Eddie stand in front of the box of wires.

"Jeez, what a mess," Eddie said. "Everything is unplugged. All those damn wires." He turned to Thor and laughed. "Spaghetti with no meatballs."

"Can you put it together?"

"Probably. Damn little I can't fix." He pointed at Thor. "Not like some others I know."

Thor was ready to bash him in the mouth, but he held back. He needed the ass to hook up the old camera security system.

If I'm right, gonna walk out of here with a fat wallet.

* * *

Dallas Dacy flipped on the flashlight and checked his cell.

Five on the dot.

He stepped through the doorway onto the second floor staircase. The scream of a mind-shattering alarm made him jump.

Damn! I forgot my electronic pass.

He turned down the stairs toward the Tunnel, but Thor and Eddie came rushing at him. Thor grabbed both his arms. "Where the hell do you think you're going, soldier?"

"I have an appointment with the administrator."

"Yeah. And I have one with the President of the USA."

"Appointment?" Eddie sneered. "At this hour? A grunt like you. In the Tunnel? Who're you kidding?"

"Check it out if you don't believe me." Dallas was trying to remain calm but he was getting really pissed.

"Ain't reveille time for a couple of hours yet," Thor said.

Eddie stood next to Thor. "Yeah, what are ya doing here?"

Norman Glick appeared at the bottom of the staircase. He looked up at them. "Take your hands off him."

Thor's arms dropped slowly to his sides.

Norman glared at him. "Come on down, Dacy. You should have taken the elevator the way I did. Less hassle."

Thor shifted his weight from one leg to another, then shoved hard at Dallas's shoulder, trying to push him down the rest of the staircase.

"No dumb vet is gonna outsmart me."

Dallas held his ground and kicked Thor in the shin.

Thor clutched his leg, grimaced in pain. "You do that again and you're a dead man." Eddie just stood there.

Dallas hurried down the steps and stood next to Norman Glick.

"Go on now," the administrator said, pointing up the staircase. "I saw the two of you come up from the Tunnel. You have no business down there after hours. For God's sake! I can smell the booze on you even from here."

Thor rubbed at his leg again, then pushed Eddie hard. "Let's move it out."

"What's the matter with you, Dallas?" Norman asked.

They were walking down the Tunnel corridor side by side.

"You're supposed to stay under the radar. Not start a war with those dumb orderlies."

Dallas was really shaken.

He'd made a simple stupid mistake all because he couldn't stop thinking about Vinnie Mazzio and his sister, and Guy. All of them had become like falling dominos. First it was Guy, then Vinnie chasing after him, and finally the sister here to save her brother. They were all going down.

Dallas had done his best to try to talk Guy into leaving Bone Point. But soldiering had sucked all the joy from the man and ECT was going to finish the job.

It didn't work out that way.

"What's the matter with you?" Norman said. "I've been talking nonstop to you and you're staring straight ahead like some dumb cow."

Dallas looked behind them to make sure Thor and Eddie weren't following.

"What the hell are you looking back there for? You think those dumb orderlies are going to cause *me* trouble"

"They're not too bright."

"Bright enough to know that one word from me to their parole officers□" the administrator sliced across his neck with a finger☐ "and it's back to a dark, dank cell. They don't want to mess with me."

* * *

Dallas shivered as he and Norman passed the ECT room. He knew in a couple of hours the techs would be getting a patient ready for the first procedure of the day.

He stopped, held onto the wall, started shaking.

His head was exploding … Afghanistan … POW … bloodied … strapped to wooden chair … head tied back … electrodes clamped to his balls ... body snapped taut … his own screams still echoed in his head.

No, no, no!

Words, off in the distance: "Hey, you coming or not?"

Dallas blinked, twisted a finger until he thought it would break.

One ... two ... three ...four ... five ... still alive.

He pushed himself away from the wall, looked down the hallway at Norman.

"Be with you in a sec."

He shuffled toward Norman.

"What the fuck?" Norman said. "Thought I'd have to send the troops after you."

Norman grabbed his arm, pulled him along, and then stopped them in front of the twin storage rooms. He punched in the code for the first room. They walked in and closed the door behind them.

* * *

Thor whispered to Eddie, "Well, you got that monitor hooked up or not?"

The two of them had sneaked back down to the Tunnel when the administrator and the vet were way down the corridor.

Eddie was deep into the wires. "Man, I'm tired. I don't do my best when I'm drunk and sleepy."

Thor snarled at him. "Quit your whining. We won't get another opportunity like this."

Eddie hooked up the discarded monitor next to the box. The screen suddenly lit up.

He broke out into a wide smile. "See? Told ya I'd fix it."

Chapter 24

Friday, 7:30 am

Gina could barely get through the rest of the night shift. She gave her report to Lena, who was back on days, and even stayed extra time to help her start her early a.m. meds before heading for the elevator. Dead on her feet, she needed sleep … at least a few hours.

She passed Thor and Eddie in the corridor. They were both unshaven, their red-rimmed eyes threw bolts of hatred at her.

Thor had just opened his mouth to say something when Delores approached.

"How was the night shift?" Delores said, cutting him off.

"About what I expected."

The nursing supervisor seemed to be studying her closely. Her smile was an unreal paste-on. "I was going to ask if you'd do one more night."

"I'd like to help out, but I'm exhausted. I need to get some rest."

Will I even be here? Not if I can grab Vinnie and run.

"Why don't we talk later? You might change your mind after you get some shut-eye."

Before Gina could respond, Delores turned and hurried away.

My God, don't any of these people take a day off?

Gina put more distance between her and the orderlies as she hurried to the elevator. Back on the fourth floor, she went to her room, checked it out to make sure it was empty. She even looked under the bed before propping the chair under the doorknob. She still wasn't taking chances with only trusting the bolt.

Then she stripped and hurried into the shower. She stood under the warm water until her legs were giving out and she couldn't stand anymore. Her back was still aching. Uterine cramping? Muscular pain from standing too long? Either could be sending up red flags for her pregnancy. She needed rest.

Maybe I should just get dressed and walk out the door.

She dried herself carefully, thinking about leaving, going home, crawling into bed, and sleeping. It was just a daydream.

Not without Vinnie. Can't leave my brother behind.

She'd packed one of Harry's tee shirts and was cuddled in it under the sheets. She held her cell in one hand and punched in his number, then disconnected before he could pick up.

There was no escaping this conversation. She had to talk to him. How could she explain everything she'd done in a way that he would forgive her?

It would have to be the truth.

Way past time for that. He'll be so disappointed in me.

She tapped in his number again. This time waited for him to answer. Instead, the answering message came on. She tried it twice more with the same results.

She closed her eyes to think about where Harry might be … and drifted off.

* * *

Donnie stared at the woman. He liked nurses. They could be mean-mouthed like Lena, but those who had worked with him when he was a patient were only tough talking. Most were kind. And Ziggy wasn't a nurse, but she was his friend.

He searched Gina's face. He'd heard her name spoken like a curse by the pair of men who wanted to harm her.

She looked sad under the glow from the bathroom light. He would stay here to make sure no one hurt her.

In the silence, explosions sputtered in his head, but they were not scary the way they used to be. Now they were far away and couldn't hurt him.

He looked through the hole again.

The nurse had come out of the bathroom, gotten into bed, and was already sleeping.

She looked like his mother, with her dark, sparkling eyes and smiling mouth. He tried to remember his mother's name. He knew he used to know it. She'd come to the hospital to see him. But when he ran away, he'd lost her.

He closed his eyes and there she was. Why couldn't he remember her name?

* * *

Vinnie was being beaten by Thor and Eddie. His face was a bloody mess☐

The bad dream awakened Gina with a start. Her back was still aching but the pain had dialed down.

She thought about what she would need to do to get Vinnie out of here. She'd hoped to talk to him, but he was so drugged up most of the time, there was nothing he could do to help her.

She remembered the holding room in the Tunnel, remembered the dead men waiting to be taken away.

It was true the men in that room had been so mentally impaired they needed hospitalization, but they were basically healthy young men. Why did they die? What exactly killed them?

And why did Guy die? That's what Vinnie needed to know, or he wasn't leaving. So, that's what she needed to know.

The death certificates! She needed to check them even though there were only few listed in the computer. Wouldn't Bone Point have an actual copy? There were none in Delores's desk or the file cabinet. The only thing of interest in her file cabinet was a folder with delivery dates.

Delivery dates? That had kept popping up in her head since she saw the folder.

Today was the soonest delivery date. But the way it was set up, it wasn't something being delivered here. It appeared that the hospital was delivering.

This hospital was failing apart, barely offering decent custodial care. But the one service they were supposed to offer was psychiatric care.

If you want to call it that.

127

What could they possibly be delivering to anybody? And according to the dates listed, they were delivering very often.

"Something's rotten in Denmark."

Chapter 25

Friday, 8:00 am

Harry had fallen in love with a rented Porsche Cayman when he'd once worked in Arizona. It had been the only bright spot during that miserable travel nurse assignment a time when he and Gina had broken off their relationship.

Gina had been terrified that Harry's life was also in danger at the time. Her former spouse, Dominick Colletti, had broken parole and was in a get-even mode. He'd blamed Gina for his having been sent to jail.

Harry had been lonely, desperate for something, anything, that would brighten his life. The red Porsche gave him a piece of joy to live for each day. He would climb into that car and chase his unhappiness down the road with a foot stomped down on the accelerator.

In a strange twist of fate, Dominick was shot and died in the ICU at the same Arizona hospital where Harry was working.

But that was in the past.

It was amazing, Harry thought, how your life could change from one moment to another … like the wind shifting or turning on itself.

Today, Harry was happy. He'd signed off on his current assignment and was going back home to his love.

He whistled with the music that blared from the radio and loved how this latest rented Porsche hugged the road during a downpour.

Despite the weather, he drove the long way back from Santa Cruz to San Francisco on the coastal highway. On and off he could see the ocean waves, high and wild and reminded him of how much he enjoyed the California shoreline.

When he reached their street, luck was with him. He found a decent parking place right in front of their building. Anxious to see Gina, he left behind his suitcase and carried a large bouquet of red roses to surprise her. He flew up the stairs and unlocked the apartment door.

"Hey, babe! I'm home."

The heavy silence was like a slap in the face.

He put the flowers down on the dining room table and walked down the hall to their bedroom. For a moment he was startled when their cat Tuva jumped onto his leg, dug her claws into his jeans. He bent down to pet her.

"Where's our lady?"

The bed was made but the drawers were open, with clothes hanging out of the sides. Basically a mess. He looked on the top shelf of their closet where they kept their small luggage.

Gone.

Right away he knew what she'd done. She was off chasing after her brother.

Worry flipped into anger that squeezed his throat until he thought he'd gag.

It was hard to wrap his mind around the fact that even though Gina had talked to him every day, she'd lied. She'd promised, promised to rest so she could get through this difficult pregnancy and have their child.

Instead, she lied to me.

He walked back to the dining room, found a vase, and methodically placed the roses into the water, one stem at a time a time.

They were very beautiful.

In one fluid motion he picked up the vase and threw it across the kitchen, screaming "Gina!" Then he laid his head on the table and pounded the sleek wood with his fist.

Tuva meowed, jumped up onto the table and licked his face. She stared at him with worried yellow eyes, her tail flicking back and forth in agitation.

He shook his head and spoke to her. "She's deserted me, too."

* * *

Helen had just finished handing out her early morning meds in Ridgewood Hospital's Internal Medicine when Harry rushed up to her. His face was a ghostly white, fixed in a mask of anger.

"Where is she?"

"Oh, Harry, I'm so glad you're here. I've been so worried."

"Not worried enough to call me or let me in on this whole thing." He moved in closer. "Not worried enough to help protect my wife and unborn child."

She couldn't stop the sudden tears that gushed down her cheek. "I wanted to tell you, but Gina made me promise not to. Besides☐"

"Besides, it was Vinnie, right?"

"It's true and I'm ashamed of it, but I needed to know someone was trying to find Vinnie. That he didn't just fall off of the face of the earth."

Harry bowed his head. "You couldn't have stopped her anyway, any more than I could have. Not unless you tied her up, blindfolded her, and beat her over the head. I'm not even sure that would have worked."

"Not when it comes to Vinnie."

He took her arm. "Is she where I think she is?"

"Yes. Bone Point."

"She's supposed to be on bed rest, not running around in a hospital. She could lose the baby."

"She won't be running around. She's the medication nurse."

He couldn't help it. He wanted to smack her. "What medication nurse do you know who just sits, and doesn't run around? And usually in circles. So you believe she'll be sitting all day?"

"I want to."

"Ok," Harry said. "Let's get back to reality."

Chapter 26

Friday, 3:00 pm

"Mr. Chavez, please come in and have a seat," Delores Smiley said, pointing to a chair. "I was delighted to talk to you on the phone and have such an experienced nurse come to work for us."

She studied the man, who moved with fluid precision as he sat down opposite from her desk.

What a mess of curly hair, but other than that he looks very presentable and professional.

"May I call you by your first name?"

"Of course. Call me Pablo."

He was extremely attentive, much more so than she was used to in the applicants who were looking for a slot in Bone Point.

"I think it's only fair to be up front with you, Pablo," she said, moving on with the interview. "This position is a short-time one. We are closing the facility in two, three months, at the latest. That's what I mean by short time."

"Ms. Smiley☐"

"Please, call me Delores."

"Well, Delores, that suits me just fine. What I'm looking for is a temporary position, something to tide me over before I leave the area. Two to three months is perfect."

"Okay, that's great. I've reviewed your employment history and you more than qualify for the position. Just for the record, let me take a quick look at your license information and I'll take you up and show you around."

"I've just packed up everything and put it in storage. Like an idiot, I stashed away my license, along with everything else.

Kind of dumb move when you're out looking for a job. But I've seen ... and done ... dumber things.

"That's okay. I'll check you out online with the Board of Registered Nursing. They'll have what I need" She raised an eyebrow. "Too bad, though. It's certainly going to cost me a chunk of time."

"I'm really sorry."

"Well, let's give you a tour of the place." At the elevator, her voice became apologetic. "The building is kind of run down. So don't expect too much in the way aesthetics or up-to-date equipment."

"I understand."

* * *

After Gina woke up, she threw on a sweater and jeans, and went to check on Vinnie. No one seemed to notice when she slipped onto the second floor.

She hurried into Vinnie's room without catching any attention. In fact, Vinnie had already taken his medications and barely nodded at her. His eyes were dull and his body was listless as he lay flaked out on his bed.

All she wanted to do was fold up and cry.

She shook her head, disgusted with herself. The worst part of her pregnancy was her body being flooded with hormones that made her overemotional. She could cry at the drop of an alcohol sponge.

Right now, she couldn't take one more second in this room.

She looked back at her brother, normally a ferocious, headstrong warrior. All she saw was a drugged-out mass of jelly.

He was not her Vinnie.

She had to get outside and away from what felt like a claustrophobic nightmare. If nothing else, she could at least stand at the entrance to the building and breathe in some fresh air.

Surrendering to her impatience, she tap, tap, tapped the button in an impossible attempt to make the elevator move faster.

Please, please, please don't let me run into those deadly orderlies.

She was ready to head for the stairs it was only one flight when she heard the car clunking along, hitting the sides of the shaft.

It finally arrived and the door snapped open.

Out stepped Delores and Harry.

Harry?

Her heart clawed at her chest. She practically bit her tongue to keep from screaming his name.

"Oh, Gina, what are you doing here, you're supposed to be off duty?

"I left something in the nurses station and went to get it."

Delores nodded and smiled. By the way, this is Pablo. He's going to work for us. In fact he'll rotate between the swing shift and graveyard shift from now on."

He's using Vinnie's counselor's name.

"H...H...Hello, Pablo." Her heart was pounding so loud she thought everyone could hear it. She held out her hand. "I hope you'll like it here."

"Hi." His blue eyes filled with tears, as did hers. They squeezed hands. She wanted to never let go.

Gina forced herself to pull her hand away. "Welcome. I look forward to working with you."

"Come along, Pablo," Delores said. "Let's get on with your tour."

Gina watched Harry until he disappeared around the corner.

* * *

Thor stood by the security camera that Eddie had repaired. He couldn't quite see the numbers the administrator tapped.

Damn, we'll need another camera hooked up from a different angle.

Well, at least that Eddie was good for something.

* * *

135

Norman and Dallas came out of the small room. Dallas was wheeling a large suitcase; he looked at his watch and knew he wasn't going to be on time for his appointment with Manky Olav at his Marin estate.

"Manky's not going to like your cutting the Vicodin supply in half," Dallas said.

"Just give him some made-up excuse, but don't tell him about our closing in two to three months."

"Hell, why not? You won't be able to hide it from him much longer. Besides, everyone knows this place is shutting down."

"But he doesn't know *exactly* when," Norman said, looking nervous for the first time. "And you're not going to tell him. That guy's like a stick of dynamite. Who knows what he'll do when he finds out."

"You can't give him what you don't have."

The lines in the administrator's face deepened. "Try telling that to him."

"Maybe you ought to make this delivery yourself."

"Sure. I'll be happy to do it." Norman gave him a big smile. "But you'd better be long gone by the time I get back." He patted Dallas's shoulder. "To the place where I found you ... on the streets of San Francisco."

"Cool down." Dallas said. "I didn't say I wasn't going to do it."

"Bet your ass you'll do it." Norman patted him on the shoulder again. "Now get going. You're going to late as it is."

* * *

Thor thought about stealing the suitcase from Dallas but he knew the guy was no pushover. He'd need Eddie's help. But the fool was upstairs taking care of the vets, covering for Thor.

Besides, all he needed were the codes and there'd be a whole lot more money. And it would be way easier than having to put down Dallas Dacy.

Chapter 27

Delores was still brooding over her meeting earlier with Norman. She hated the way he demeaned her nursing career, her wanting to get back to staff nursing. The one thing she'd always been proud of was being an RN.

Who the hell does he think he is? He may be my cousin, but he's also really nothing more than a broken-down MBA.

She remembered when this whole thing began and he dragged her down into it. It sure wasn't her idea to start collecting drugs from dead veterans, sell them to the drug cartel.

Right from the beginning, ten years ago when they started working on their first hospital revamp and closing, she'd complained to him. "I don't get it. Why are so many of our patients dying? It's downright ghoulish."

He'd looked uneasy. "Patients die. Nothing unusual about it."

"Maybe they're sick, mentally unstable, but you don't die from being crazy unless you kill yourself. We're going to have to dig deeper, check with other VA hospitals ... find some answers. It's true we're here to close this place, but patients are supposed to transfer out ... not die."

"They died. Let it go at that." His face flushed and he looked away from her. But his whole body language shouted that there was something wrong.

"What are you hiding from me, Norman? Does this have anything to do with the sloppy updates on our computers? Most of the dead patients are still listed as active on our census rolls."

He sat and stared at her.

"Think about it, Delores. Really think about it and you'll figure it out."

The truth would never have dawned on her.

Instead, she'd made it her business to check the stats in the other VA hospitals across the country, the psychiatric stats specifically at poor-performing VA hospitals. Their morbidity rates were way lower than Bone Point's. Way, way lower.

One day he sat her down in his office.

"Stop kicking up a fuss, calling the other hospitals. You're going to cause us trouble. These people are dying because we're killing them."

"What do you mean … killing them?"

"Delores, you really are dense." He barked out a laugh. "Maybe that's why I wanted you in the first place."

She stood. "Now wait a minute."

He held out a hand. "Just pushing your buttons."

She was ripping mad. "I think you need to explain yourself, Norman. Now!"

"Don't you get it? This is the reason I pushed to work with these substandard facilities. There was no way we were going to improve them. Did you really think we would … or could?"

"Probably not … but—"

"I knew there was a way to put them to good use from the moment we walked through the door. Yeah, we put on a good show, but with that first step into the building, the hospital is doomed."

Delores just stared at him.

"Come on. You've known that right along."

"Known what?"

"When these facilities perform poorly, we're simply going to shut them down."

"Okay. Maybe that's a good thing. Now the vets will finally have their problems addressed. We both know how the government has been cheating veterans. They need better care."

"Maybe that's your interest, Delores. It isn't mine."

Delores knew she wasn't going to like what she heard next from Norman. Maybe somewhere in the back of her mind she'd always known but had only seen what she wanted to see.

"What *is* your interest, Norman?"

"M-O-N-E-Y."

"They must pay you one hell of a salary."

"There you go, being dense again."

"Okay, that's enough." Delores said. "I'm entitled to the truth. I have a license on the line to protect. Just spit it out or I'm leaving."

"We're taking those vets out for their drugs, but we keep their files active so the central pharmacy keeps supplying us with their drugs."

"Taking them out?"

"Finishing them off."

"You're kidding me. You're *killing* them for that?"

"Don't look at me that way. Most of them aren't redeemable anyway. Only a bunch of crazies … a burden on society."

She remembered that day very clearly. It was the day she willingly aligned herself with a premeditated murderer, making her one too.

* * *

When she'd learned the truth, she should have walked out instead of pocketing the cut she started to get from the sale of the drugs.

The whole thing was a nightmare. The hospital continued to collect drugs on ghosted patients even though they were really "gone."

She got up and paced around her small office.

Norman and Manky had been working together from the beginning.

When they stopped delivering the drugs, Manky Olav would come after Norman Glick. And Norman probably wasn't the only one.

He'd come after her, too.

Chapter 28

Friday, 3:00 pm

In one smooth motion, Allison York methodically pushed in her thumb drive. She'd learned a long time ago to back up every computer report with a portable drive. Watching others get burned with disappearing information had convinced her that she was never going to be one of those people.

She brought up the Bone Point file.

The Inspector General agent took a moment and leaned back into her desk chair and looked at the silver framed picture of her family. It sat on the corner of her desk next to her prize calendar.

She was teased about her old-fashioned calendar where one numbered paged flipped to the next number of the month.

Nothing but a space and dust collector.

But it was a daily reminder that time is the most precious thing she had. It could be lost in the blink of an eye.

Just like her brother … gone in the blink of an eye.

The Bone Point file had grown in the past month. If it wasn't for her informant, the administrator and nursing supervisor at that institution might have gotten away with their whole operation. And the two of them had already closed two other hospitals.

History:
Ziggy Jones, informant, anonymously contacted IG's Veteran Affairs office six months ago with her observations and complaints. At first she refused to be identified or engage in a personal interview. However, she finally was interviewed by Agent Allison York, who had been assigned Case #6627.

Informant, Ziggy Jones: Sole remaining receptionist at Bone Point Hospital.

Alleged Charges:

Ghosting Patients Stealing Benefits: Current census of fifteen patients. Accessed official records: sixty patients. Confirmation pending.

Physical Abuse: Patients beaten and neglected by staff orderlies. Confirmation pending.

Murder: Ghosted patients listed as discharged were killed. Confirmation pending.

Drugs: Sale of patient drugs. Confirmation pending.

Allison tapped into Administrator Norman Glick's short profile: In his late fifties, single, lives at the hospital. Job qualifications: MBA Verified

She glanced at his picture. Brown eyes, brown hair, average-looking middle-aged male with no outstanding identifying facial markings.

Nursing Supervisor Delores Smiley profile: Mid fifties, widow, lives at the hospital. Job qualifications: BNS Verified

Allison looked at Smiley's picture: Brown eyes, blonde hair, average looking female. No outstanding facial identifying markings.

If you'd met these two at some kind of gathering, nothing about them would capture your attention. But the Inspector General's agent had found in her limited experience that evil doesn't always mark a face, even though it always destroys a soul.

As if these vets haven't suffered enough, now they were being tossed into a meat grinder to make sure they're completely torn apart.

"Hey, Allison, how's it going?"

"Hi, Isaac." He'd startled her. She could feel herself blushing, just as she did every time she looked at the gray-eyed, wavy-haired agent. Looking at him gave her goose bumps.

"I'm really looking forward to our dinner tonight," he said.

"Me, too."

He waved and took off.

She'd sworn she'd never date another agent, but somehow the two of them had clicked from the moment their hands touched in an introduction. It didn't take long before they were dating and falling into bed together. The love word hadn't been spoken aloud but Allison was thinking it.

She forced her head back into the job: Bone Point.

In two months they would close the hospital and these suspects might vanish. Oh, what they did *might* remain behind them to mark who they were, but Allison wanted *them,* wanted to catch *them* red-handed and on the job. She wanted *them* to pay for what they'd done. Revealing records, verbal condemnations wouldn't be enough, as far as she was concerned.

She wanted those Bone Point criminals to rot in jail.

Chapter 29

Friday, 6:00 pm

Two of Manky Olav's guards thoroughly searched Dallas Dacy's rental car and the large suitcase filled with drugs before he was allowed to drive through the ornate gates of the estate. To top it off, they'd also patted him down from head to toe, not being any too gentle about it.

After driving to the parking area, Dallas stayed in the car until the dogs were called off. Then he was escorted through lush gardens to the front entrance, where he was searched again. He'd expected it. These were the usual redundant security checks every time he delivered drugs.

Grin and bear it.

He lugged the large suitcase up a grand staircase, each step cut from beautiful marbleized stone. He knew Manky didn't drag himself up these steps. He rode an elevator to the second floor. Dallas had been on it the original time he came with Norman to be introduced to the hotshot.

As he walked up the steps, he fantasized about what *he* would do with the kind of money Manky made.

First of all, he'd take care of his mother and father so they wouldn't have to worry about putting his sister through college. Beyond that, he knew he wanted to go back to school. Get a real education and maybe become a doctor.

Thinking of that always made him feel good.

The doctor who took care of his arm when he was living on the streets became an example of someone who he'd want to be like.

Time to stop these crazy thoughts. All they did was make him realize how little he really had. Besides, right now he had all he needed. And he didn't have to use the San Francisco streets as a mattress.

By the time he got to the top of the stairs, he was covered in sweat and the suitcase felt like it'd gained twenty pounds. Another guard stood on the second floor waiting for him. He led Dallas into Manky's office. It was a large room with expensive furniture and colorful oriental rugs. The drug czar's desk seemed to be swallowed up by the rich brocaded drapery behind it.

"I expected you an hour ago."

Dallas rolled the suitcase up to the desk. "Sorry, traffic was a bitch today."

Manky was dressed in charcoal wool pants with a tan tee shirt that clung to him and emphasized his toned body. He stood and came around the desk and nodded for one of the men to open the suitcase.

Dallas stood off to the side. He knew exactly what was in there. He and Norman had crammed it tight with the bottles and packets of pills. There wasn't extra room even for a bee's tongue.

It was all labeled:

Antidepressants   Prozac, Zoloft, Paxil.
Anti-anxiety   Klonopin, Valium, Xanax, Ativan
Opioids   Vicodin, Percocet
                   –
Amphetamines   Adderall

Manky rubbed his palms together like an old man getting ready to dive into a huge feast. Then he fingered the few opioid packages on top lovingly. "Yes, yes! These are like gold on the street."

Dallas nodded.

"Are the rest of the Vicodin and Percocet on the bottom?" Manky said.

Dallas could feel the acid growling in his stomach. "No. That's all we have this time."

"I see." The drug czar said. "And why is that?"

"Some of the orders must have been delayed."

Manky nodded to the guard, who closed up the suitcase and wheeled it out of the room.

"Come, come, sit while I get the money for Norman." He picked up his desk phone. "Bring us some vodka." He listened. "Yes, yes, for two."

"So, Dallas, how does Norman treat you? Does he take good care of you?"

"I'm not complaining."

"Good answer." Manky steepled his fingers under his chin. "You know, we could use a good man like you." He laughed. "Especially one who doesn't complain."

Dallas smiled and nodded. "I gave up guns when I left the military. I think that's probably a requirement for your job."

One of his goons came in with a tray holding two very elegant cut-crystal, gold-rimmed shot glasses. Dallas had never seen anything like them. A bottle of vodka was open and ready to pour. He could tell it was Russian by the name, but Dallas had never heard of it.

Manky poured into the glasses and offered one to Dallas.

"*Zdarovye!*"

Dallas held his glass up. They tossed back their drinks at the same time. He was immediately buzzed.

"So, Dallas, I've been hearing a rumor that Bone Point is closing. Going out of business. Is that true?"

"Yeah, it's no secret. It's going to close."

"And when is that?"

"That would be a Norman question. I don't know the answer."

"Something tells me you do know the answer."

"Have you talked to Norman about it?" Dallas said, starting to feel this was going somewhere he didn't want to go.

"Norman will tell me what I want to hear. I'm looking for the truth … from a man who can't complain."

Manky reached for the bottle and poured them each another drink.

147

"*Zdarovye!*"

Dallas downed the drink and stood. "I think it's time I got Norman's money and drove on back to Bone Point."

"I don't think so," Manky said. "Sit down!"

In no way was it a request.

Chapter 30

Gina took the elevator down, waved at Ziggy before she stepped outside through the front entrance. At any minute it was going to rain again, but for now only heavy gray clouds hung low in the sky. It had rained the whole time she was at Bone Point, like some constant celestial warning for her to leave the place.

But for the first time in days, Gina felt safe.

She took a deep breath. Today, nothing horrible would happen to her baby … would happen to her.

Harry was here.

And she didn't need to lie anymore to the person who meant the most to her.

She would be working the night shift, Harry was working the swing shift. Their paths would cross, but she needed to wrap her arms around him now, this very moment, if only to know he was real.

And she needed to talk to him. Really talk.

Her thoughts were interrupted when Delores and Harry walked out the entrance.

"Getting some fresh air?" Delores asked.

"It's nice to be outside." Gina spoke to the nursing supervisor but she only had eyes for Harry.

"We'll see you tomorrow, Pablo," Delores said over her shoulder as she went back inside.

Gina's heart was racing. She and Harry stood face to face.

"If you ever do that again, Gina, I swear I'll pull your hair out, one at a time."

"How did you find me, *Pablo*?"

"You know how," he said.

"Helen."

"Of course. She's worried to death, not only about Vinnie, but you, too. She also told me you were using your married name. Pablo suggested I use his name."

Oh, those blue eyes. She wanted to grab him and squeeze him, never let him go, but someone inside might see them.

"I'm sorry. I couldn't tell you. I knew you'd try to keep me from going. And I had to find my brother." She leaned harder against the wall. "Did you see him?"

"Not yet. He wasn't included in the grand tour."

"He's terrible. Drugged out of his head. They're all drugged. Not only that□"

"Gina, we have to get away from this place. There's nothing we can do here, and most of all, you're supposed to be resting … not running around hospital units."

"I know. But if we don't get Vinnie, they're going to kill him."

"Kill him? Come on, Gina. Why?"

"No! Listen! I met one of the patients in Vinnie's room before they killed him. He died last night. I saw his dead body. Him, along with two others. It gets worse."

Harry was getting agitated. "How much worse can it get? We've got to grab Vinnie and go … now!"

"There's more to it than that."

"Tell me!"

At that moment the skies opened up and unexpected hail battered everything. It stunned the both of them for a moment

"You must have driven up here. Where's your car?"

"You can see it from here."

She looked across at the open parking lot. "You didn't," she said.

"Yep, I held onto the cute little Porsche I rented to go to Santa Cruz."

"Let's sneak up to my room, sexy man, I'll clue you in on everything I know."

"That's the best invitation I've had in days."

She gave him an evil glare. "It better be." Then she was smiling. "Now that Ziggy's seen you with Delores, she won't try to stop you. Take the elevator to the fourth floor."

Gina waited a couple of minutes, went back into the building and headed for her floor.

* * *

Donnie was lying on his bed looking at the pictures he'd collected and pasted up on the walls. He wished he had electricity to see everything at once, but he could only shine the flashlight on one image at a time. He especially liked the pictures of the mesas in New Mexico. At least that's what it said next to the photos. All that space. He wanted to be in all that space so he could dance and spread his arms wide and hold it all.

Everything in the pictures looked familiar to him, or at least made him feel warm and like he belonged. He could imagine the smell of the dry air mixed with the odors of farm animals. Sometimes he imagined himself running after goats.

He pulled his special basket close to him and fingered the treasures within.

There were bright colored buttons he'd found in a box on the deserted women vet's floor. Also in the box, a lock of red hair and a bar of soap. With painstaking exactness, he'd carved a woman's face in the soap, one that he remembered as his mother's. But what he loved the most was a hawk's tail feather. He didn't remember how he'd gotten it, but it made him feel warm and safe when he held it. No one could hurt him then.

He touched everything and hummed a song that he knew his mother used to sing to him. She would rock him back and forth and hum a wordless song, but it spoke of the wind and the rain sweeping across the land. He didn't know how he knew that, he just did.

* * *

The elevator door closed. Gina and Harry stood motionless, face to face, eyes locked on each other. And then they were in each other's arms.

151

"Oh, Harry, Harry! I was afraid I'd never see you again." She covered him with nonstop kisses on his neck, face, and then their lips met.

"How are you, doll? Tell me you didn't hurt yourself." He squeezed her tighter. "Tell me everything is all right with our Baby X."

"We're really good now that the three of us are together again."

When the elevator opened, she took him by the hand and hurried him into her room. "If Dolores finds us together, there'll be a lot of explaining to do."

She locked the door and placed the chair under the knob. "There isn't much time before I have to do the night shift."

"Hey, so a lock isn't really enough?" They both sat on the bed.

"Did you meet the orderlies, Thor and Eddie?"

"Yeah, I met the goons. I could see they're nothing but trouble." He wrapped an arm around her shoulder, looked into her eyes. "Have you had problems with them?"

"I've managed to keep them at bay. So far. But they're really dangerous men." She felt sick to her stomach. "I think they're the ones who are killing the patients."

"But why? What do they have to gain?"

"I'm not sure yet. But I do know the VA is closing down this hospital in two or three months."

"I know that, too. Delores mentioned it when she hired me. That still wouldn't explain why they would want to kill their patients."

"I haven't pulled it all together yet, but I'm scared to death that Vinnie is next.

* * *

The hermit watched the woman and the man through his hole in the floor.

He knew the two of them belonged together. This man wasn't trying to hurt her. He had his head on her naked belly and seemed to be listening. This must be the father of the baby.

Donnie wanted to hear what they were saying to each other, but there was only a buzz of meaningless words that he could hear through the thick floor.

He watched the man touch her with such warmth and love; tears welled up and flowed down his cheeks.

He wished he could be loved like that.

Chapter 31

Friday, Manky's Compound, 7:00 pm

Dallas's ear was buzzing like an angry hornet. He wanted to reach out and swat at it, make it stop, but he couldn't get his hand to move.

He tried to open his eyes but only one would unsnap and then everything was a red blur.

What the fuck is going on?

Then he remembered. One of Manky's goons had moved into his space, just as casual as can be, and clobbered him alongside the head. Hard! He'd seen an array of colors before everything went black.

Now everything from the neck up was throbbing to the beat of his heart.

Gaboom, gaboom, gaboom.

Damn, just what I was afraid of. All I thought about sitting there and drinking that vodka was that they're going to work me over until I tell them what they want to know.

"Well, well, boys. Look who's almost with us again."

He recognized Manky's voice, with its extra slimy friendliness.

Yeah! Friendly as a black mamba. Damn, I wish that buzzing would stop. If it keeps up much longer I'm going to barf.

Dallas lifted his head and a sharp stab pierced his eye. "Hey, Manky, I don't want to complain, but what's the deal?" He held out his wrists, bound with plastic zip-ties. "One minute you want me to work for you, the next, you tear my head off."

Manky laughed. "Yes, I can really see you're not a complainer. Hey boys, take off the wristees ...let the man move around."

Dallas still could only see out of one eye and that one gave him only a blurry world. He watched the smear of two men snip the plastic ties from his wrists. He rubbed at each wrist until he could feel the blood filling up the numbness.

"Wa ... water."

"Give him some water. The poor man can barely speak."

One of the goons put a full bottle of water to Dallas's lips. He drank it all.

"Now, you know I like you, Dallas," the drug czar said. "This is nothing against you. But business is business. I need to know what's going on."

"What do you want to know?" Dallas wished he could have another bottle of water. "I'm just a messenger boy."

Manky wagged a finger back and forth. "You're not a boy, Dallas. You're a veteran. A soldier. I respect you ... don't disrespect yourself."

Dallas was starting to see clearly out of the one eye.

Manky pointed to a chair and one of the goons scraped it across the cement floor. Manky gave him the evil eye and the man picked up the chair and carried it the rest of the way to him.

The moment gave Dallas a chance to look around. He was in some kind of cellar, with a naked bulb hanging from the ceiling. It was eerie and it smelled bad. Also hanging from the ceiling, about ten feet away, was a meat hook, and under it, spread on the floor was a large sheet of plastic,

Shit! This guy's going to kill me if I don't give him what he wants.

Manky sat down and scooted up close to Dallas.

"I don't want to hurt you, man. Your work has been outstanding and you've been reliable, someone I could count on. I know this probably seems unfair to you. But I've got to know what I've got to know. I'm just a businessman who needs the kind of information that will keep me in business."

"Then why have me hit on the head? My ear is still buzzing."

156

"Is that a complaint? Dallas?" Manky said, with a bark of a laugh.

"Just a fact."

One of the goons walked up to Dallas and punched him hard in the jaw. Manky held up a hand to stop the next blow.

"When is that hospital closing?"

Dallas was silent, trying to fight the pain that crippled his mouth as he moved his jaw around.

"Dallas, don't you get it? You seem like a smart man. I'm only going to ask you one more time before we move you to that meat hook and hang you by your skin. Then we're going to hack you to pieces, a little at a whack, so by the time you tell us what we need to know ... and you will ... you won't care if you're alive or dead."

Dallas looked at him with his one eye.

Manky's voice was very soft. "Exactly when is the hospital closing? When will my supply of drugs stop?"

The vet told him everything.

Bette Golden Lamb & J. J. Lamb

158

Chapter 32

Earlier...

On the patient unit, Thor watched Eddie clomp down the hallway like some hick turned loose in a cow pasture. The guy had no style. Just a back-country hillbilly.

Thor couldn't imagine how he ever got hooked up with that loser. But Thor had to admit that Eddie saved his ass in lockup too many times to count. The man had a helluva fist.

"Where've you been? All you had to do was set up another camera. I should have done it myself." Thor looked at his watch. "You've been gone over an hour."

"Took me some shuteye. Man, I'm beat."

"Didn't you take the uppers I gave you, you dumb boob?"

"Yeah, I took them," Eddie said. "Still, if you knew shit about putting anything together, you'd know it takes time."

"I could do it if I wanted to." Thor turned away from Eddie. Could barely look at the guy. "Anyway, is it working?"

"We'll be able to see the code keypad when Norman uses it again. Then we'll get the stuff and hit the road. Man, I can't wait to get clear of this place."

"I've been thinking about that, too," Thor said.

"I'm not ever working in a hospital again."

"Did you see the new *nurse* they hired?" Thor asked. "Pablo something, just another fuckin' Mex."

"Yeah, I saw him. Pansy-assed boy nurse."

"Pansy ass or not, the dude looks like he could hold his own," Thor said

"No boy nurse is ever going to get past this." Eddie flexed his arm and his muscles bunched up.

"Anyway, I like it better when they're women. At least there's some potential for some body work." Thor elbowed Eddie. "Did you get it? Body work."

"Yeah, I got it. How dumb do you think I am?"

"I'm still gonna nail that Gina bitch, her and that stupid New York accent." Thor could feel the heat building up in his gut, just the way it did every time he thought about getting messed up by her, then her getting away.

Thor reached out and shoved a patient when he stumbled a couple of feet in front of him.

"We had that girl trapped." Eddie said. "I still can't figure out who that dude was who slammed us."

"Long as I get her in the end, I don't give a rat's ass."

"Well, I do," Eddie said. "I don't like people popping up and jumpin' on me. No one gets away with that."

"Well, looks like this one did, *superman.*"

Eddie's face turned bright red and he clammed up.

They'd long finished the cleanup job of the vets messy beds and scrap papers and shit scattered everywhere. It had been a few hours since they passed out their lunch trays. This was the time the two of them laid back and goofed of if they could get away with it. And they did most of the time.

"Let's do some planning," Thor said.

"What planning you talking about?"

"You are the dumbest dude I've ever met." Thor leaned back against the wall, disgusted. "Getting into those storage rooms with the double security number pads, you fool. What else?"

"You call me dumb. We don't even know what's in there." Eddie laughed. "It could be filled with a shitload of bedpans." He thought that was funny, roared with laughter. "Boosting that would not be a money maker. I'm sure as hell not risking my parole for that."

"Didn't I promise when we got out that we'd never go back again?"

"Uh-huh! It was you and that last job mess-up that got us nailed. That jewelry store gig is what landed us in the slammer." Eddie's face was red and all scrunched up like it always got when he was pissed.

Thor wanted to bash him in the face. His hands had balled into fists that he kept pressed to his sides. "Not my fault the security guard got the drop on us shot you, tasered me."

"Yeah, yeah." Eddie said. "Heard all your stupid excuses before. Didn't change nothin'. Three years in a cell is more than I can take. I'm not ever going back to prison."

"We may not know if there's anything worthwhile in those closets, but I'll bet my last dollar it's gotta be good."

One of the vets was pushed by another guy. He landed smack up against Thor.

"Hey, you. What in hell do you think you're doing?"

"Sorry, man."

"You that Vinnie something? Bed buddies with Rick Bell and Dallas Dacy?"

The man looked at him with blank eyes. "Yeah, I guess."

The guy could barely stay upright. "Get out of here." Thor gave him a hard push. "I still can't get over it. The military kicked me out but kept someone like him. Does he even look like a real soldier?"

Eddie was silent.

"I asked you a question?"

"I don't know … these guys are so messed up … being a soldier doesn't even come into play anymore."

Thor picked at a thumbnail for a long time. When he finally spoke, he had to fight to keep from yelling.

"Let's make some plans to get into those closets. After this is all over, you and I are splitting and I don't ever want to see you again."

* * *

Vinnie struggled away from the crazy orderly. There was definitely something wrong with the man.

161

His head was spinning and he could barely keep his eyes open from all the drugs he'd been given. Lena had started checking his mouth again to make sure he took his meds and he had trouble remembering why he even came here. Why *was* he here? He thought for a while.

I've come to find out why Guy died.

Yeah.

What have I found?

Nothing.

All Vinnie could picture in his head was quicksand. That's what he'd done to himself. He'd jumped into it, was stuck, and he was going down.

And now Gina was here, too. All he wanted to do was cry.

Chapter 33

Friday, 9:00 pm

"Get down here. Now!" Norman roared into the telephone.

"What's going on?" Delores said. "I just got back from dinner."

"Never mind that, just get down here."

When Delores opened the door to Norman's office, he yelled, "Where the hell is he?"

"For god's sake, quiet down!" She slipped into the chair opposite his desk. "Who are you talking about?"

"Dallas!"

"Dallas?"

Norman eyed his watch. "He should have been back here by now. Something's wrong. I know it."

"Maybe he took some time off … it could be any number of things." But she felt a sudden chill start at the base of her spine, curl up and around her neck. She stopped, placed a hand on her forehead. "Oh, for a moment I forgot he was delivering the goods to Manky today."

"Forgot? Are you kidding me?"

"Well, I don't deal with that part. It's your end of things."

"Is that so?" He gave her a nasty pasted-on smile. "Seems to me you're in the thick of it when you snatch up that wad of money we receive every week."

"You know exactly what I meant, Norman. Don't get huffy with me because you're worried about Dallas." But she was worried, too. "Did you try his cell phone?"

"Two or three times. It goes to message."

"Do you think Manky would harm Dallas?" She was getting more uneasy by the minute. "I mean, he just delivers the stuff … only a go-between."

"Who can tell what the hell Manky will do? He's a stone-cold killer. Would you rather he came after you and me?"

"Could you call Manky? See if he got the product. Let him know you haven't heard from Dallas … then at least we'd know the vet hasn't run off with the money."

"The less I have to do with that man the better. But I see no way out of it."

"Let me know what happens." She stood and headed for the door without another word.

* * *

Norman glared at the closed door and picked up the receiver for his landline, slammed it down without punching in Manky's number. He swung his chair around, stood, and paced around the small office.

What was he going to say to that killer without ending up taking a beating himself?

Hey, Manky, I've been wondering how you took the cutback on the Vicodin and Percocet?

But he had no choice. He went back to the phone and tapped in the code for Manky's private line.

"Norman! Hello! I thought I'd hear from you sooner."

"Did Dallas get the goods to you today?"

"Like clockwork."

"Well, I was getting antsy. He should've been back here by now."

"You know how it is. We got to talking and time whizzed right by."

"I see."

Manky laughed like he'd just heard the funniest thing in the world. "I don't think you do see."

"What's that supposed to mean?"

"When were you going to tell me that your nut hospital is going to close soon?"

"I just figured as long as you were getting the product, what difference did it make."

"You see, that's the point." Manky's voice had gone from lighthearted to morose black. "I didn't get it all today, did I?"

"I gave you what I could."

"Uh-huh. And what if I only gave you the money that I could? You wouldn't like that, would you?"

"Look, I can't give you what I don't have."

"Yes, that is a good answer, Norman." There was a long silence. "I have given Dallas half the amount you expected to line your pockets with."

"Now wait a minute. I gave you more of other drugs to replace the missing opioids. That should have worked."

"Worked? No, it didn't work," the drug lord said. "I have commitments to my line of suppliers and a whole chain of workers. As a businessman, I think you understand what I'm saying."

"Look, things are getting tight here. I'm dealing with logistics. I can only get so many drugs for so many people. You understand?"

"You mean so many dead people, don't you?"

Norman hadn't fooled this crook for a moment. Manky had obviously figured out exactly how Norman was getting the drugs and how and why the quantities were going to slide.

"What do you want me to do? I don't need the VA or the DEA sniffing around. Once the feds get involved, I'm finished. Records will have to match, I□"

"Stop whining! I don't give a royal shit about how you do what you do. Either get me all my drugs or you get … I think you know what you'll get. Just ask Dallas when he shows up."

With that, he disconnected.

* * *

Every muscle, every joint, every inch of Dallas screamed in pain as he drove back to Bone Point. He could barely hang onto the wheel. It took everything he had just to keep going through the motions of driving.

He knew he'd been lucky to get out of Manky's compound alive. The man had made it very clear, that if Dallas didn't answer every question he was asked, he would be cut into pieces and thrown away. Nothing but dead meat.

And for what? Norman Glick?

Norman and Delores? They were just the flip side of Manky. Better trappings of civility, but just as murderous and crooked. Dallas knew their shtick. Knew what they were doing. They were not only stealing drugs, they were murdering vets.

Men and women like me served our country only to be ignored when the military was through with us. Nothing but throwaway trash.

And those crooked administrators got away with it by manipulating a bureaucratic system to homogenize the whole mess and profit from it.

Well, Dallas was finished. Maybe it was better to live on the streets than have any more to do with these murderous bastards.

* * *

Dallas limped into Bone Point Hospital. Before he could get on the elevator, Norman was headed toward him, and not walking, but running.

"My office. Now! We need to talk."

"Norman, I need to go lie down."

"Not yet."

Dallas followed him, limping down the corridor, but once inside the office, he collapsed into a chair. He could barely breathe and his heart was skipping beats.

"You look terrible."

Dallas could feel Norman studying him for a moment more before turning away and staring off into space. "Tell me what happened."

Dallas wanted to jump across the desk and choke the man, choke him until he was dead.

166

"What happened?"

"Manky's men worked me over, but good. They beat the shit out of me ... that's what happened." He rubbed at his jaw over and over. Dallas knew he was lucky it wasn't broken. "It was supposed to be a warning for you. But you look just fine. There you sit, not a scratch on you while I was taken down to within an inch of my life."

"I'm really sorry, Dallas. I didn't expect this."

"Yes, you did. You knew exactly what was going to happen."

"I didn't think they'd do *that* to you."

"What the hell did you think he was going to do when you shortchanged him?" Dallas tried to shift in the seat, but it hurt too much to move. "All you care about is yourself. The rest of us are collateral damage."

Norman turned beet red, barked out a laugh. "Do I care what you think of me? You and all the rest of you are just broken clumps of humanity."

"We are now."

"Oh, please. Don't tell me you didn't know what you were getting into when you signed up for duty. But you wanted the sign-up bonus. Just like you knew what you were getting into when you came here." Norman couldn't suppress a sneer. "When I picked you up you were nothing but a down-and-out street bum, begging for pocket change."

"You keep throwing that up in my face. But do you know what it means to get literally dumped because you've become a shell- shocked, unemployable statistic?"

"It's a sad story. But I've heard it a million times since I got into this line of work."

"Do you even know what these vets have gone through? Do you know what it's like to see your best buddies die before your eyes?"

Norman shifted in his seat. "I don't mean to be insensitive, Dallas," he said in a matter-of-fact tone, "but that's not my problem."

Dallas lifted himself from the chair. He had to get out of there. Every part of his body was knifing him with stabbing pain.

"No. That's true, Norman. But every vet here is *supposed* to be your problem. You're *supposed* to help heal them. Isn't that what Bone Point is *supposed* to be about."

"Now you're telling me my job?"

"That's right, I forgot. I'm just a bum with no resources. A bum who can do nothing to you."

"Best you remember that."

Dallas knew his eyes held the hatred he felt. "I can't hurt you in any way … that's true. But Manky? That man will not only cut your heart out, he'll make sure you're staring at it until the moment you're dead."

Chapter 34

Earlier...

Harry was a few minutes ahead of time when he arrived at the nurses station for his first swing shift at Bone Point. Delores was supposed to meet him there, but she hadn't shown yet. He said hello to the a.m. nurse through the barred window.

"Hi, I'm Pablo Chavez, the new p.m. nurse. Delores was supposed to meet me here but I'm a little early. You're Lena Rossner?"

"That's right. And I've been expecting you. Delores sent an email about you, Pablo. Come around to the door. I'll let you in."

Harry walked up to the locked door and waited. Lena opened it and held out a hand. She had a firm grip but her smile was tentative.

"We haven't had any new blood in here for a year. Now in one week we have you and Gina Lucke."

"You sound disappointed."

"Not at all. It just seems strange."

They were interrupted by Delores, who unlocked the door and came in.

"Good afternoon. Pablo, you beat me here. I wanted to introduce you to Lena."

"Oh, we slid through all the preliminaries without too many difficulties." Harry smiled at both women.

"Well, there isn't too much to reveal here. Basically, you'll be the meds nurse, like I said earlier. That's how this hospital manages the majority of patients that have PTSD."

"No psychiatric backup of any kind?"

"Most of the vets who arrive here need inpatient custodial care and have already been through the whole shrink process *ad*

169

nausea. But they do have periodic psychiatric evaluations. At one time we had in-house docs, now we rely on visiting teams. But most of our treatment consists of applied behavioral therapy with medication or ECT."

"ECT? That's a rough therapy to undergo."

"We've had some good results with it."

"I'd heard this hospital treats female vets."

"Did treat. They've all been transferred out already because of the closing."

Delores seemed uncomfortable now.

But he watched Delores run through her spiel like she'd done it a million times, as if she was talking about rocks rather than suffering veterans. Before this, he'd held his feelings about her in check, but now he knew he didn't like her.

"Well, if you don't need me anymore, I'm out of here," Lena said, smiling.

"I think Pablo will have no problem handling the unit. Right?" Delores said.

Harry nodded.

"Oh, the orderlies will be on duty for another couple of hours, so they can assist you if you need help."

"Right. I think I can work my way through most situations." Harry smiled. "But thanks."

* * *

Harry set up the meds in a short time. The men were lining up outside the window when he opened it.

When Vinnie stood in front of the window, they stared at each other for a moment before Harry gave him an empty cup. "Down the hatch, Mazzio."

Vinnie looked at the empty medicine cup, pretended to toss the contents into his mouth, and gulped down the offered water.

"Okay, next," Harry said.

Vinnie stepped away, smiling.

When Thor, Eddie, and Harry finished handing out the dinner trays, the two orderlies started down the corridors.

"Good night, sucker," Thor yelled out.

Eddie just gave Harry a stupid grin.

* * *

When it was after 10:00 pm and Harry was convinced most of the vets were out cold, he headed for Vinnie's room.

His brother-in-law jumped off his bed and they gave each other a bear hug. When they separated, Vinnie's eyes were welling up with tears.

"Really glad … you're here ... man … so worried about Gina … know she's had problems … been no help to her." He pointed to his head. "The meds☐"

"It's okay, man. Gina's fine and we're both here for you. We're going to get you out of this nightmare."

"First time I've been able to put thoughts together … in days."

"You didn't *have* to take the meds."

"Man, you don't know what you're talking about. Tried not taking them. Those goons☐"

"What goons … the orderlies?"

"Yeah, them! They got me into restraints, beat the shit out of me." Vinnie looked away. "There is no such thing as not taking the pills. Got away with it only twice before. Once with Gina."

"I'm sorry, Vinnie."

"Harry, you've got to check out my roommate. Dallas Dacy. He's been beaten up, looks awful."

"Yeah, sure. Did Thor or Eddie hurt him?"

"He won't tell me anything."

* * *

Harry stood over Dallas's bed. He looked down at the shirtless man, who was covered in tattoos that contrasted with vast areas of purple hematomas. Harry could tell his nose broken, and the bruising around his chest made him think Dallas probably had some broken ribs as well.

Jeez, what a mess.

171

Harry pulled a chair close to the head of the bed. Although Dallas's eyes were closed, Harry sensed he was awake.

"Hey, man. Why don't you let me check you out?"

Dallas's eyes snapped open. "Are you a new goon they hired?"

"This is my brother-in-law," Vinnie said. "You can trust him. I swear."

Harry took the stethoscope from around his neck. "Okay?"

"I've got banged-up ribs, bruised kidneys, and my nose is probably broken. Trust me, I've had worse. But go ahead, satisfy yourself."

Harry helped him sit up, noticed the massive scar on his arm as he listened to his chest, heart, and lungs. Then he checked his nose. "You're right on with your diagnosis, Dallas."

"Yeah, been there before. Don't even think about pain meds. I'll make it through without that poison."

"If you let me, I can help get your nose straight, and I can see you're having trouble breathing because of the pain from your ribs. It's hard to tell if they're broken without an X-ray and there's no tech here at after five. But nothing seems out of alignment. If I tape you up, it might let you get some deep breaths and cut down the pain."

The hard glint left Dallas's eyes. "Thanks, man."

"Who did this to you?"

"I asked him, too," Vinnie said. "He wouldn't tell me."

"Look, you two, I appreciate your help." Dallas grimaced as he tried to shift his position. "But trust me, the less you know, the safer you'll be."

Chapter 35

The hermit tried to read again. The words in the magazines he'd stolen over the years were hard to understand, but every day Donnie kept trying. He could sound the words out easily because they had a familiarity that he knew he should know. But the sounds only brought shadows of those memories.

Words that began with B upset him.

Bang. Blast. Bullets. Bomb. Beheaded. Blood.

Those B words made his head rumble, no matter how they were used.

Visions of men being shredded by bullets, splatters of blood after loud bomb blasts. Beheaded brothers who were soldiers, like him … beaten.

When he saw those things in his head, he would cover his eyes and cry.

Sometimes he cried all day long.

* * *

Gina tried to get comfortable in her jeans, then she finally gave up and unbuttoned them. She used a large sweatshirt to cover her bulging middle.

Soon nothing will fit.

She glanced at the time. She'd be going on duty soon.

She needed to go back down into the Tunnel before her shift started. There had to be something she'd missed the last time she was there. Something she hadn't seen or noticed.

A part of the equation was missing.

She had to get her brother out of this place. But she knew he wasn't leaving without answers to Guy's cause of death. Right now, she couldn't think of anywhere else to look except the Tunnel.

On her side, the orderlies were now off duty and hopefully had gone home.

If not, she would be ready.

She took the pepper spray and Swiss Army knife from her purse and shoved them into separate pockets of her jeans.

I may be nuts for doing this, but I gotta do what I gotta do.

She'd been to the morgue and seen the dead men; she was almost sure they were murdered. If so, Guy must have died the same way.

Murdered by whom? Why?

Thor and Eddie? *They* took Rick Bell away. And he died.

If the orderlies were murdering the vets, did they plan to murder everybody over the next two months? As brainless as those two were, they were, they wouldn't be doing it on their own. The administrator? Delores?

The answers had to be in the Tunnel.

"Baby X," she said, patting her belly, "you and I are on our own."

* * *

Gina stepped out of her room, locked the door, and turned. A man with a startling white beard was standing about ten feet away staring at her. Her heart hammered in her chest and she could barely breathe. There was nowhere to go … he was blocking the staircase exit, and her door was locked.

With one hand, Gina covered her belly. The other was in her pocket clutched around the pepper spray. "What do you want?"

"I won't hurt you … I promise. I only wanted to say hello."

He was big and muscular, but his body language was childlike: humble, wanting to be liked. What finally calmed her were his eyes. They were soft and questioning, not aggressive.

A sudden flash of memory made her focus on his white beard.

Was this the man who saved me from being raped by Thor and Eddie last night?

"What's your name?"

174

He shifted from one foot to the other before he said, "Donnie."

"Donnie, you're not a patient here, are you?"

At first the man looked bewildered. Then he shook his head very slowly.

"Were you a soldier? Did you have a bed here?"

He nodded, pointed to the ceiling.

"Where do you live?"

He pointed to the ceiling again.

Swallowing hard, Gina moved closer, held out her hand. "Hello, Donnie. My name is Gina."

He tentatively touched her fingers and pulled back.

"Why did you help me last night, Donnie?"

He thought a moment before he pointed her belly. "A mother. No one should hurt you. I won't let them."

"Thank you." Gina smiled. "Well, I'm hoping to be a mother in four months." She patted her belly, noticed she'd been doing that more and more since the baby started kicking.

Donnie wanted to talk, she could see that, but either he didn't have the words or he was too frightened. She wasn't afraid of him anymore. He was more like a confused, lost child looking for help.

"Do you want to see my pictures?"

"Are they up there?" She pointed at the ceiling.

He smiled and took hold of her hand and led her to the staircase.

This does it. Everyone who's called me crazy over years is right. What am I doing?

He took her arm and helped her up the steps. She knew he would have carried her if she asked him to. He was like a gentle giant.

On the fifth floor she started to reach for the light switch, but he said a soft "No. They can't know I'm here."

"Maybe they'll help you."

"They will take me away and I'll *never* find my mother."

"Your mother? Where is your mother?"

175

A sudden gush of tears covered his cheeks. "I don't know. I've lost her."

Gina took his arm and squeezed it. "Don't cry, Donnie. We'll help you try to find her."

A genuine smile cut through the tears, revealing coated teeth that hadn't seen a toothbrush for a long, long time.

"This way." He took her arm and led her through the shadowy abandoned floor. The only light came from widely spaced windows that splashed an eerie luminescence here and there across the concrete floor. Donnie seemed to know every step to take to avoid the debris left behind when they vacated and shut down the floor. All the room partitions had come down and were gone.

All but one. It was propped against a wall.

Donnie took her hand and walked her inside his space. He pulled a flashlight from behind something and turned it on.

The space came alive with beautiful colors from glossy strips of magazines. On top of the torn out pieces were pictures of sunsets, oceans, canyons, forests. And on top of those were pictures of children with their mothers, holding hands, smiling, happy.

"Donnie, this is beautiful. Do you have a picture of your mother?"

His legs seemed to give way and he dropped down to the floor.

"No," he said, looking up at her. "I lost it. It's gone. She's gone."

Chapter 36

Friday, 10:00 pm

Thor and Eddie stood in front of the two storage rooms where Norman had *something* stashed. Thor's total focus was on the locked doors. They had to find a way in. For once in his life he might have hit it big.

Thor punched in the numbers he'd recorded seeing from the extra security camera Eddie had installed in the ceiling.

Nothing happened.

He tried the same numbers again.

Still nothing.

He stabbed the numbers again,,

"Why the hell doesn't it open?" Thor snapped.

"Are you sure you got the numbers right?" Eddie said.

"All three times, damn it." Thor's stomach was turning. "Why doesn't it open?"

"Maybe Norman resets the numbers every time."

Thor growled, "Well, wouldn't you see that on the camera?"

Eddie glared at him. "I don't know. Maybe he resets it from inside."

Thor could see Eddie didn't like the way he was talking to him, but Thor was mad at the jerk and he didn't care what he thought. Things never seemed to go right with him. There was always some kind of fuck up.

"What about the other one?" Thor said.

"What about it?"

"You are so fucking dense. I'll bet you have trouble finding your way out of bed in the morning."

"You shut your mouth," Eddie said. "You've done nothing to try to make this happen other than yammer at me. I'm the one who does all the fixing, makes things work. What have you done?"

Thor laughed. "I'm the one who does the thinking, you fool." He stared at the set of numbers for the other door.

Eddie glared at him. "Face it, man. You're the one who don't know shit."

Thor slapped Eddie's face, followed with a hard punch to his belly.

The jerk clutched his gut and collapsed.

Thor looked down at him, still hot and angry. He wanted to kick Eddie in the head. Before he could do anything else he heard voices moving in their direction.

"Shit, it's Norman and Delores." He grabbed Eddie by the belt and hoisted him up. "Try to get your act together, man."

* * *

Norman was startled to see the orderlies standing in front of his stash rooms. "What are the two of you doing down here?"

Neither of them said anything.

His surprise turned to disgust. "Am I invisible? Can't you see me? Hear me? What are you doing here☐"he looked at his watch☐"off duty?"

Delores leaned into Norman, said, "Leave them alone."

"Leave them alone? No way. I want an answer. Now!"

"It's pouring out," Thor said. "Nowhere for us to go … we're just walking the halls for exercise. That's all"

"I don't believe a word you're saying, Thor. Is he telling the truth, Eddie?"

"Yes, sir," Eddie said in a flat voice. "We're just looking for exercise and this floor is a good one for running up and down the halls."

"The Tunnel is not a playground," Delores said.

Norman was still fuming. "I find you here on this floor one more time without a solid reason, and I mean one relating to patients, you're out of here. Get me! Out!"

"Yes, sir," they said in unison as they turned around and walked away.

* * *

Thor whispered in Eddie's ear, "Let's get to the security closet."

They hurried to the closet at the other end of the hall where the controls and the monitors were. The two of them could barely fit in the small space together, but they didn't dare leave the door open. Thor didn't liked being that close up to Eddie. He smelled like slimy, old sweat.

Inside, they both stared at the screens. It was soundless, but the cameras showed that Norman and Delores were arguing.

"Wouldn't you like to be a fly on the wall there?" Eddie said.

"Only if they're talking about the codes to get into that sucker," Thor said, pointing at the places where something was hidden.

* * *

Donnie, holding his bag, took Gina's hand as they walked down from the fifth floor to the Tunnel. He was the one who was childlike, yet, the way he was trying to guide her made her feel like a little girl again. It gave her a strange feeling of humility to know all of us are only one step away from total dependence on someone else.

Donnie whispered, "No talking. We have to be very silent." He patted her on the back to reassure her.

In the Tunnel, Gina heard Norman yell out, "Get out of here!"

Donnie gently tugged on Gina's hand and led her down the corridor a short way to the kitchen. Inside, he pulled her to the end of a long counter, where the dinner trays were still stacked. He stooped down; she did the same. He held his forefinger to his mouth for silence. But no one came down the hall that Gina could hear. Whoever was supposed to leave was probably still here in the Tunnel.

* * *

179

Thor whispered to Eddie, "Look, he's hitting the numbers. Let's write them down. He pulled out his cell and punched in the numbers in his contact space. "Damn, this is fun!"

Eddie whispered, "Not if we get caught."

"Oh, don't be such an ass. We're not going to get caught. We're gonna get rich."

"Can you see what's in there?" Eddie said.

"Almost, until they closed the damn door."

"Well, hell, I need to get out of here," Eddie said. "I don't like being wedged into small spaces."

"You're not the only one." Thor cracked open the door. "Now! Let's go!"

* * *

Gina heard the stairwell door shut. So did Donnie. They both stood. But Donnie still held his finger to his lips. He picked up his cloth bag and moved to the pantry. He began filling it with canned stuff. He selected just a little of each kind of food. As she watched him, she wondered how long he'd been living and hiding like this.

Was he even a veteran? He must be. This place was too far off the beaten track for him to just happen on it.

She'd heard the fifth floor, where Donnie was living, was the first part of the hospital to empty out. It had been a women's unit. So he'd probably been on his own for at least three years. At some point he must have been a patient here. Maybe there was some kind of record of his existence. Maybe they could find his family.

Donnie tapped her shoulder, held his finger to his lips again.

* * *

"I don't care what you say, those orderlies had no business being down here. And they were standing next to our stash," Norman said.

"Why waste your time worrying about those two idiots?" Delores said.

"Why waste my time? Are you kidding me? Manky Olav is on the war path. I'm trying to save our necks. That guy is going to kill us."

180

"Okay, I get that," Delores said. "But why does Thor or Eddie pose any kind of threat? Don't we have enough problems without looking for more?"

"You really are being obtuse."

"Hey, don't pull that on me." Delores said. "You keep telling me everything is as much my problem as yours, so spit it out!"

"Look. Those guys might be idiots but if they found a way to get into our supply … you can forget about going back into nursing or doing *anything* ever again. Got it!"

* * *

Now that everything was quiet in the Tunnel, Gina and Donnie stood.

Gina patted her belly for the umpteenth time that day and wondered what Norman Glick and Delores Smiley were hiding in the bottom floor of Bone Point.

Just another complication added onto the reason Gina was here in the first place: What happened to Vinnie's buddy?

Were the two things even tied into each other?

And was she ever going to get her brother out of this hell hole?

Chapter 37

Friday, 10:30 pm

Manky Olav paced back and forth in his office, stopped at the window to look out at his massive lighted swimming pool. It had stopped raining and staring at the velvety turquoise water was hypnotic. Maybe he'd take an hour or so and go for a late swim.

The woman he'd been sleeping with for the past week was stretched out nude on a chaise lounge. Her sensuous breasts shifted slowly as she turned on her side, sending a sudden spike of heat flashing through his groin.

Yeah! A swim would feel good right about now.

He flipped his attention to the men who were supposed to be guarding the perimeter. They had eyes only for the nude woman.

In an instant, he had his cell in hand and punched a single number. Less than ten seconds later his right-hand man, Hernando, burst into the office. He looked around puzzled.

"*Jefe, que pasa?*"

"I'll tell you what. Bring your ass over here and see what I see."

His head man looked out the window and smiled. "Yes, she has a beautiful body."

Manky's voice was low and rough. "I ought to burn your ass."

Hernando's eyes grew large. He fingered the scar on his face.

"Look again! And this time you'd better tell me what's wrong out there." Manky pulled a gun from his desk and pointed it at Hernando.

His face blanched and he seemed to have some difficulty breathing. He turned back to the window, only this time he never looked at the woman as he searched the area.

"*Madre de Dio!*"

"Exactly. Now you'd better take care of that situation. And it can never happen again or instead of a quick shot to the head"□ he lifted the gun□"I'll hang you by your balls from a meat hook."

Manky slipped his gun into his pants behind his back.

"*Si, Jefe!*"

Hernando hurried out of the office. The next time Manky saw him he was standing outside his window. A smile tugged at Manky's lips as he watched Hernando pull his weapon and shoot the four men with dead-center head shots. They never saw the attack coming□ they were still busy looking at the woman. They hardly had a chance to hear anything. When they did it was too late.

Hernando was not only accurate, he was fast.

He saluted Manky through the window, and then picked up the screaming woman and carried her away from the pool area. He brought her in to Manky, who took her into his arms.

"It's okay, baby. Don't worry. Everything's good."

"That man killed ... killed those men."

"I know," Manky said. "He was only protecting you."

She had calmed down but she was still whimpering.

"Shush ... shush...shush," he murmured in her ear.

When he felt her going limp in his arms, he reached back into his belt, pulled out the gun, and shot her through the head.

He lay her down on the Persian carpet and swatted at the massive splatter of brain tissue that covered his shoulder where her head had been resting.

Hernando rushed into the room. "What happened, boss?"

"She saw too much to live. Now get her out of here."

* * *

Manky left the office and went to his workout room. He went through his routine, from lifting weights to running on his treadmill. By the time he finished showering and returning to his office, there wasn't a trace of the dead woman's body.

Bone Point

His biggest problem was going to be replacing the four "trusted" men.

His private number buzzed on his cell. He looked at the caller ID carefully. Yes, he'd been expecting this call. He took a deep breath before he opened the line on speaker phone.

"Tommie, glad to hear from you. How's it going?"

"How's it going? You goon, you know exactly how's it going."

"All right, I'll get you your stuff. My supplier is having some problems."

"You think I give a rat's ass about his problems? I got problems of my own. One of them is not getting the goods to the customers."

"Look, I'll have it for you in the next couple of days," Manky said. "Will that do it?"

"Yeah, that'll work."

Manky could tell there was more.

"You've always been reliable, man, Manky … don't start disappointing me now, 'cause you're not the only supplier out there, ya know."

Manky's neck stiffened. "Your family's been dealing with us since my grandfather ran the operation. One small hitch and you're threatening to walk?"

"Yeah, yeah, I know. You and me go back a long way. But business is business. I need the goods or my distributors look to the other suppliers. Where the hell do ya think that's gonna leave me? Up shit creek. That's where."

"I'll have it for you by tomorrow night, Tommie, even if it is Sunday. Will that do it?"

"Don't let me down, Manky." With that he clicked off.

Manky was fuming. He thought about rubbing out Tommie for giving him so much lip.

But then he remembered what his grandpa always said: "When people do the right thing always be decent." Tommie was a whiner, but a good friend. Manky could afford to be decent.

* * *

Manky lifted his cell and tapped in Norman's number.

"Hello, Norman."

"Hey, Manky. What's up? It's after hours and I'm laying back a little."

"You know, Norman. I don't give a fuck that it's *after hours.* In my line of work, which is really your line of work, we work twenty-four hours every day."

"No, I get it. I'm just surprised."

"Well, I've got a bigger surprise for you. I want the rest of the order you stiffed me on … immediately."

"But☐"

"Don't *but* me, Norman. This has to be made right. Otherwise, it's your ass that's going to get reamed."

"I'll get it to you."

"Damn right you will. Not only that, I want a shipment every other day for the next two months. Hear me."

"I can't☐"

Manky disconnected.

Chapter 38

Friday, 10:45 pm

When it was time for Gina's graveyard shift, she arrived several minutes early so she could talk to Harry. He unlocked the door to the nurses station and pulled her into his arms.

"Hello, beautiful. I've been waiting to do this."

"Well, hello, Mr. Lucke, or is it Mr. Pablo Chavez?" She laughed. "Does this mean I'm having an extramarital affair?" She looked coyly at him.

"Long as it's with me you can call me any name you want, you little trouble maker." He held her at arm's length and looked into her eyes. "You look a little more rested. Have you taken a nap?"

"More like being relieved to have you here. But I did lie down for a while."

"Proud of you."

"Harry, I've been dying to tell you something really fascinating."

"Oh, Gina, you can't imagine how nervous I get when you say something like that."

"No, this really is fascinating. I met a vet who's living in the building *sub rosa* on the fifth floor."

"No one knows he's here?"

"No one. It seems he was a patient at one time and ran away. But he can't remember names and details of his family, so he obviously has no place to go. He sneaked back in again and has been living on the deserted fifth floor ever since."

"That's really something. He must be pretty self-sufficient."

"He sneaks food from the kitchen at night and he collects stuff patients leave behind." Gina looked away. "I didn't want to tell you about it before, but he saved me from being … raped the other evening."

"What? Raped?" He squeezed her arms, pulled her up tight against him. "Why didn't you tell me about it before?"

"I didn't want you to freak out. Anyway, Donnie bushwhacked them. And I got away."

"Donnie?"

"That's the hermit's name," Gina said. "When you meet him, you'll see that description fits him to a tee."

"Haven't heard the word hermit used in a long time," Harry said.

Gina nodded. "Anyway, I was lucky he was there."

"Doll, you know I love your brother, but *you're* the most important person in the world to me and I need to settle this. Who was it? Who tried to hurt you?"

"It didn't happen, Harry. That's what counts."

"Whether it happened or not, this is no place for you and the baby. I want you out of here, right now."

"Huh-uh. No way!"

He hugged her tighter.

"I don't give up on the people I love."

"I know that, but☐"

"Right now," she said, "we have to concentrate on what happened to Guy so we can pull Vinnie out of here and leave. That's what's important. Have you had a chance to talk to my brother?"

"Without the drugs clogging his mind, he makes a lot more sense. Seems he's been scouting on his own, but he's so exhausted that even off of the drugs, he needs a lot of shuteye. I just left him. Let him rest."

"Something is going on in that Tunnel. When I was down there with Donnie, I heard Norman and Delores talking. They must have something illegal stashed in the storage rooms. I think the orderlies were someplace around there, too. Hiding."

"Answer me. Are they the ones who tried to hurt you?"

"Harry, please drop it. I'm okay. Isn't that what matters?"

"It is and it isn't. You can't be the same old feisty Gina you're used to being. Not if you want to have our baby."

"You know how I feel about the baby, but☐"

"Gina, there are no buts."

"Well, there's nothing I can do right now. I'll be stuck in the nurses station for the night, and the on-call tech signed out sick. I don't dare leave the patients alone. Maybe you could look around." She took his hand. "Please?"

"Okay, I'll go down to the Tunnel, see if there's anything I can find."

She looked into his eyes and smiled. "I love you, blue eyes." She leaned over and kissed each eye before she kissed his lips. "You be careful. Remember, you're going to be a dad."

* * *

Thor and Eddie were back at the storage rooms now that the two bigwigs were gone. Thor was tapping his foot as Eddie tried the last numbers they'd seen Norman use to gain entrance.

"Nope, it's not working," Eddie said. "I don't know what he's doing that we're not picking up on." He looked closely at the security box. "Damn it!"

"Hey, what do you see? What are we missing?"

"I don't know why I didn't see this before. Looks like this flat place is the right size for a thumbprint." Eddie stuck his thumb onto the area above the numbers.

"There's gotta be something we can do," Thor said. "I'm not letting this slip by. I know whatever's in there is going to make me rich."

"*Us* rich. You keep forgetting that."

"Yeah, *us*."

A voice behind them called out: "What are you two doing here?"

Eddie froze.

Thor turned around and saw the new nurse, Pablo Chavez. "Just messing around."

Eddie was silent.

Pablo looked at his watch. "At this time of night you're messing around?"

Thor said, "Well, what in hell are you doing here, and what do you care?"

"I came down to check out the ECT equipment … not that it's any of your business."

Thor didn't like this newcomer just walking in and bossing them around. He wanted to smash his face, but he wasn't about to get into any kind of to-do when they were about to pull off a big heist.

"I think the two of you better take a hike."

"Yeah, we were just going anyhow," Eddie said.

Thor didn't say anything, but his eyes were shooting flames.

* * *

Harry knew these two had to be the ones who attacked Gina. It was either them or a couple of vets. Pretty much all of the vets, though, were too drugged up to even begin to think about sex illicit or otherwise.

When the two orderlies were gone, Harry moved to the storage rooms and examined the security boxes the orderlies had been messing around with.

Vinnie, you dog, what kind of mess have you gotten us into?

* * *

Thor and Eddie rushed down the hallway to the out-of-sight security closet. They squeezed into the small space and turned on the monitors. Pablo Chavez was still standing in front of the storage rooms. At first he just fingered the code boxes. Then he took a couple of steps back and stood there, arms crossed.

Thor said, "He's gonna try to steal our stuff for himself."

"Naw, he's just sizing it up. That's all." Eddie elbowed Thor. "Stop breathing on my neck."

"Shut up. I don't want to be jammed in here anymore than you do." Thor pointed at the screen. "We're getting into those storage rooms tonight."

* * *

Thor and Eddie watched Pablo's every move on the monitors.

"Why is the dude just standing there?" Eddie asked.

Thor pointed to his own head. He's thinking. You know, using his brain unlike some others who don't even have one."

Eddie stood up taller. "You shut your mouth. I've about had enough of you."

Before Thor could respond, Pablo stepped away from the storage rooms and moved out of view of the camera. Thor cracked open the closet door and listened. Soon they heard the stairwell door close. They stepped out of the closet; both of them were covered in sweat.

"Where are your tools?" Thor asked.

"In the janitor's compartment at the other end of hall. Jeez, you've seen me go in and out of there a million times."

"Shut up and let's go get what we need to get into those storage rooms."

"If we find anything worth some bucks, where are we going to stash it until we can get it out of here?" Eddie said. "If you're the big thinker, you better come up with an answer or I'm not breaking into *anything*." Eddie crossed his chest with his arms. "I'm not going back to jail."

"We're *not* going back to jail. What we're gonna do, is be rich."

"You're going to feel pretty stupid if all we find are some linen supplies." Eddie laughed, seemed to find that very funny.

"Sure, sure. When have you ever seen plain old sheets locked up tighter than a drum?" Thor was pacing in a small tight circle. "Let's get what we need and get started."

"Stop giving orders. I'm not your slave."

"Oh, shut up and let's go get the stuff."

* * *

Eddie and Thor made a pile of the tools they thought they would need to open the storage rooms, plus a long extension cord for the electric drill and reciprocating saw.

"This is too much to carry all at once," Eddie said in his whiney voice.

"Thought you said there was a flatbed dolly in here," Thor said. Where the hell is it?"

"Loading dock!" Eddie shouted. It has to be there."

"Will you keep your voice the fuck down?"

Eddie ignored him and started for the doors leading out to the loading dock…and there was the dolly.

"Okay, you happy now, wimp?" Thor said.

"Look, man, that 50-foot, multi-outlet extension cord alone would have done me in."

"Like I said, you're a wimp."

They loaded everything onto the dolly and took off for the security rooms.

"What time you got?" Thor asked Eddie, noticing the dude did look pretty bushed.

"After two. It's getting late."

"That means we just have to move it along," Thor said. He was excited. He knew they were about to make a real killing.

Eddie started sawing immediately around the security box. The wood wasn't dense, but the metal plate holding the box took some time. Finally, he removed the box and its holding plate, exposing a set of wires.

"What're the wires doing?"

"We just hit gold."

Eddie took a pair of clippers and cut one of the wires. The storage room door unlatched with a soft click.

Thor and Eddie looked at each other, stunned for the moment. Then they pulled at the door and it opened.

"Jesus Christ! Will you look at that."

All Eddie said was "Yeah." Drool was running down his chin.

They stepped inside and caressed the large, opaque white, plastic bottles of bulk drugs and boxes of smaller quantities, all neatly lined up and labeled.

Thor said, "You want to bet there's more of the same in the other one?"

"Man, I gotta admit, if we can move this stuff, we're in the big money."

Thor nodded. "Let's get to the other one."

* * *

In a few minutes they had the second storage room open.

"Look at that," Eddie said. "You were right; it's another stash of drugs."

"Yeah, told you so, you dumb shit."

"Where the hell we gonna to store all this stuff?" Eddie whined and glanced at his watch again. "Like, we need to hustle, get it all out of here."

"Yeah, this is going to take some time with that slow elevator and everything. We sure as hell don't want to still be doing this when the food supplier gets here with the prepared breakfast trays."

Thor eyed Eddie. His head was spinning, trying to think. "Let's put it up on the fifth floor. That area has been closed for ages." Thor rubbed his hands together.

"Yeah! That's a great idea," Eddie's face was red with excitement. "It's gonna take at least four trips even with the dolly."

"Well, let's get a move on."

Eddie pulled a small plastic bag from one of the boxes, zipped it open, and popped a couple of pills into his mouth.

"Hey, cut it out. We need to keep it neat or it's just gonna be a big mess of pills. Remember, we have to sell that stuff before we see any money."

Eddie stopped, turned to Thor and gave him a high five. Some of the pills scattered when he tossed the bag back into the box.

Thor let out a small whoop, then quickly crossed his lips with his finger for silence.

* * *

It took more than three hours for Eddie and Thor to transfer all of the drugs from the storage rooms in the Tunnel to the fifth floor.

"Man, I need something to eat," Eddie said when they were finally finished putting away the tools. Let's go get some shit from the vending machines in the break room."

"You gotta be fuckin' kidding me," Thor said.

"No, really, man, I'm starving."

"What if someone sees us, wants to know what we're doing here this time of night?"

"Like *who*, for shit's sake? Ain't nobody around at this hour 'cept that pregnant bitch on the patient floor. If anyone does get nosey, we'll say we stayed over because of the rain. Besides, we've done it before, so who'll give a fuck?"

Thor nodded. "Let's go get some crap out of the machines and grab some shut-eye."

"Yeah, those uppers stopped working hours ago."

Chapter 39

Saturday, Early Morning

Delores kept tossing and turning. She just couldn't sleep. All she wanted to do was get up, pack her suitcase, and run. She tried to remember what exactly got her involved with Norman Glick in the first place.

I suppose greed is the ultimate answer.

But it was more than that. At one point, when they first started working together, ten years ago, she'd been attracted to him, even though he was a cousin.

But that was when she was still wide-eyed and trusting. Not that she really saw herself that way. She was an experienced nurse and had seen enough of life not to be easily fooled.

Yet, she was.

Now she let reality slip into the basic truth of their relationship. He'd needed her, used her attraction for him, and her loneliness to rope her in.

Still, she couldn't blame it all on him.

She'd been a willing partner, wanted someone to love, but at the same time, wanted the VA hospitals to fail. He wanted a medical professional to help him shut down and steal from the underperforming hospitals.

He used her managerial skills to collect the drugs that kept flowing in even after a person was dead; she helped him to lie, to ghost the dead patients. She knew bureaucracy even better than he did.

And Delores had been the one to make all the records make sense. She was responsible for picking out the sickest of the hospital patients and having them finished off.

A chill rode her body when she remembered that Norman originally wanted *her* to murder the patients to keep it totally secret.

She'd refused.

Maybe there was hope for her. She wasn't *really* a murderer.

But she arranged for them to die. She was the one to give the orders.

Yes, she really was a murderer.

At the first couple of hospitals they'd managed, she'd told herself the suffering vets were better off dead. No more hallucinations of killing or being killed. No more nightmares, no more panic attacks, no more PTSD. No more pain.

She bought into the lie for a long time, but at Bone Point she began to see that they were just really killing people for money.

No wonder she wanted to be a staff nurse again. She could get back to helping people. Or at least that's what she told herself.

Delores swung her feet around and got up from the bed. She looked out the single small window that served the two tiny rooms that were hers. Right now it had stopped raining and a crescent moon was peeking through the surrounding clouds. It gave off a very small glow of light.

She walked to the corner desk and sat down. Searching through the two drawers, she came up with some fresh paper.

She wrote down the whole scheme, confessing her part in the operation, listing all the names of those involved. When she finished, she folded the papers into an envelope and addressed it to Ziggy Jones, the only person she trusted to do the right thing. She would put it in Ziggy's desk early in the morning.

Feeling much better, she crawled back into her bed, but the first thing she saw when she closed her eyes was Manky's snake eyes staring her in the face.

* * *

Dallas wanted to turn over, but he didn't dare move. His ribs were throbbing and his face was burning from the open wounds. Manky's thug had clobbered his face while wearing a school ring.

The ring had caught Dallas' attention the first time he was slugged. Being beaten by a college graduate seemed bizarre.

He had to get away from here. It had only been a need for survival that made him take the job in the first place. But it was way past time to move on. He'd had enough of the Normans, Deloreses, and Mankys of this world.

He listened to Vinnie mumble in his sleep, repeating the name *Helen* before he was finally silent.

Vinnie had jumped into this hellhole only because of Guy's death.

In the short time Guy was here, Dallas had gotten to know the man pretty well. At least as well as you can know a bummed out veteran who'd lost everything that was ever dear to him.

* * *

One night Dallas stopped Guy from banging his head on the wall, and asked, "What are you doing, man?"

"I'm trying to make it all disappear."

Dallas pressed a torn bed sheet to Guy's head to stem the bleeding that just wouldn't stop."

"The memories?"

"No. The pain from the memories." Guy pounded on his chest over his heart. "It hurts. You hear me? It hurts so bad." Tears ran down his face. "I want to die. That's all I want."

Dallas put an arm around his shoulder. "You need some help, man. Someone to help you move on."

"Don't you get it? There isn't anyone."

* * *

Dallas thought about those times with his roommate. Guy would lie in his bed with his eyes searching the ceiling.

What was he looking for? What kind of answer did Guy expect to drop from the heavens when everything else around him was failing?

Dallas wondered if there was a God. And if there was, why did he allow such suffering to haunt even those who believed in his existence.

197

Guy was religious. He prayed at his bedside every single night that Dallas could remember.

Maybe having someone else murder him *was* granting his prayers.

Maybe.

Dallas remembered the night Thor and Eddie pushed Guy onto a gurney. Dallas wanted to stop them. He knew what was going to happen, where they were taking him, what they were going to do to him. But Dallas just lay in his bed with his eyes closed and let them go without saying a word.

Dallas shifted and turned on his side. He bit his lip and tasted blood to keep from screaming in pain from every part of his body.

If there was a God, Dallas knew he was receiving just a taste of the punishment to come.

Chapter 40

Donnie heard the men rummaging around at the other end of the floor. His inner clock told him it was early morning, the time of day when the enemy had attacked before. He started shaking, knew they'd be coming soon. He huddled in his warm blanket, tried to make himself tiny; he needed to be small to keep them from finding his hiding place. He felt around for his weapon but without his flashlight, he couldn't find it. He didn't dare turn his flashlight on.

I don't want to die. They'll kill me if they find me.

The voices sounded familiar but the old fear of being trapped and killed kept him pinned to his mattress. Bad men were out there, that he knew.

He would stay quiet and remain safe.

But the noises in his skull were louder than ever before. He hit the side of his head against the floor until they stopped. Pretty soon he fell back to sleep.

When he awakened, he remained perfectly still and listened until he knew he was alone again.

Maybe it had all been a dream.

He fell back to sleep again and when he finally got up, he quietly walked down to the bathroom. He looked in the mirror at his white beard and once again thought that he must be very old.

When he was cleaned up, he put on his clothes and looked through the hole in the floor. He watched the woman crawl into the bed with the same man who seemed to love her very much. Right now, they were hugging and kissing. He turned away and decided to walk down to where he thought he'd heard the noise earlier.

It had been a long time since he was at this end of the fifth floor. He walked carefully, remembering that he'd fallen over a fragment of old inner wall. He still had the scars where the wood tore into his skin and ripped out a chunk of muscle.

He stopped to look out one of the windows. It was daytime and the rain was still pouring down. But he felt warm and protected in his own little hiding place.

He almost forgot why he was at this end of the floor. He rarely walked this far away from his spot.

Turning, he fell over a bunch of piled-up stuff. He hadn't seen it. Dark blankets covered several large piles. He flipped one blanket away.

Donnie had never seen so many big bottles of pills in his life.

Then he knew why the voices in the dream sounded familiar. They were from the two men who worked in the hospital. The ones who always hurt people, were going to hurt the nurse.

Some of the bottles were piled on a dolly. He grabbed the handle and carefully pulled until the wheels started turning. It took him several minutes to take the dolly to his end of the floor.

Donnie immediately began unloading the drug bottles from the hand truck and stacking them in one of the old bathrooms. Sweat dripped off of every part of him, but he knew he had to hurry and finish getting all of the drugs before the men came back.

He didn't know how long he'd been working. It just became a simple rhythm of load the dolly, bottle after bottle, pull the load to the other end, then unload bottle by bottle, box by box until they were all moved.

He used the blankets to cover up everything, then took the empty dolly back to where he'd found it and left it there.

* * *

Saturday morning, near 8:00 am, Delores went down to the office, saw Norman was already there. She went in and plunked herself on the visitor's chair, and glared at him across his desk. She waited for him to speak first, but he stayed silent. She lost the battle, couldn't stand the tension in the air anymore.

She said, "You know, Manky almost killed Dallas. That poor man is in terrible shape."

She didn't like the way Norman was looking at her. He had that crafty, what-can-she-do-for-me leer.

"I want you to deliver the rest of the drug order to Manky today."

"Are you kidding me? It's Sunday, damn it. I don't want to even be here with you."

"Actually, I'm very serious. Dallas certainly can't go. That leaves you."

"Really? I think *you* better get ready to move it out because I'm not going anywhere near Manky."

"He's not going to hurt you. All he wants is his Vicodin."

"It's almost humorous how you manage to get everyone else to do all the dirty work while you hide in the shadows. Not going to work this time."

"Well, what good are you if you can't help out with the very thing that brings in the money?"

"I'm the one who runs the hospital, the one who covers your messy tracks, makes sure the bureaucratic machine doesn't wipe you out."

Norman swiveled in his chair, probably so he could look out an imaginary window and try to figure out what he was going to do.

"We got to do something. That drug czar wants his product today. And we both know if we don't make sure he gets it … he'll kill us just as an example, if nothing else."

"Well, you take care of it because I'm finished with all of this."

Chapter 41

Saturday, 9:00 am

Norman sent for Dallas. He sat at his desk, coffee cup in hand. He needed the caffeine; he'd barely slept at all. Even though this was his second cup in the last hour, his eyes still felt like billiard balls.

Thor wheeled in Dallas and left without a word. Norman studied Dallas sitting across from him. He'd hoped not to involve him anymore, but there was no one else. The vet was having trouble even sitting up in the chair.

Dallas looked like one huge, moving purple bruise: two black eyes, a taped up nose, fiery cuts across his cheeks and jaw, and to top it off, a split lip that made Norman cringe.

He looked worse today than he did yesterday when he first came back from the drug czar. Norman could only imagine the kind of severe damage the man had under his clothes.

Manky's men had really worked Dallas over. Norman couldn't help it, his stomach was clenching, sending bolts of pain across his gut just looking at him.

Better him than me.

The administrator hesitated. Delores had turned him down, but he didn't think Dallas had the same option. Still, asking him to go back to Manky with the rest of the delivery seemed crazy.

But it was pure self-preservation. Norman wasn't putting one foot into Manky's compound.

No one's going to use me for a punching bag.

"Manky wants us to deliver the rest of the drugs today," Norman said.

"I'm sure he does."

"Will you complete the order?"

203

"Think I'm some kind of fool? Look at me. I'm not going anywhere."

"You know I have to get the rest of the delivery to him. And he wants it today."

"You couldn't fill the order yesterday. How you going to do it today?"

"I'll take some from the current supplies."

Dallas's mouth hung open. "You mean you could have had the whole order and you didn't send it?" The vet's face turned ashen. "If there was a way to do it before, why didn't you?"

Norman just sat, looked back at him.

"You son of a bitch!"

"And who the hell do you think you're talking to like that?"

"I'm talking to you. The one who's responsible for me getting trashed. Answer my question. Why didn't you send the full delivery yesterday?"

"You know our last in–house doc left us, and now some of the visiting docs have been cutting back on their Vicodin orders. I was just trying to get Manky used to it."

Dallas went silent, tried to reach for his cup of coffee on the edge of the desk, but it was too much effort. He gave up, fell back into the chair.

Norman got up, came around the desk, picked up the cup, and gave it to him. Dallas took it and sipped it very slowly as though the heat hurt his lips.

"Do you really know Manky?" Dallas asked.

"No. I took a steam bath with him when we first met. And I had just one brief meeting after that. Let's just say, I didn't enjoy his company either time."

"Did you know his family have been drug lords for three generations around here, maybe even longer?" Dallas took another sip of coffee and leaned the cup against his chest.

"Of course I know. They run the Bay Area's underground drug operation like a well-oiled machine."

Bone Point

"Then you've made a deal with the devil," Dallas said. "When you tell him you're going to deliver, you'd better deliver. I don't care whether it's drugs or pizza."

"Come on, Dallas, you and I have a solid deal … let's not mess it up."

Dallas shook his head, leaned forward, set the cup back on the edge of Norman's desk, and lifted himself painfully out of the wheelchair. "I'm not going back to Manky ever again. You can throw me out, Norman. I don't give a shit." He limped to the office door, tossed back over his shoulder, "Just remember, I know where all the bodies are buried."

"Are you threatening me, Dallas?"

"Take it any way you want." He slammed the door behind him.

* * *

Harry showed up at the nurses station around nine.

"What are you doing here now?" Lena asked.

"Couldn't sleep in that crummy motel," Harry lied. "Figured I'd follow you around for a little more orientation."

"You won't get paid extra for it, you know."

"Didn't expect to be."

Lena started putting the a.m. meds together, explaining to Harry at the same time how the order for drugs was filled by a central VA pharmacy in San Francisco.

"In the last three years, they've started to deliver them in bulk quantities. When the drugs arrive each month, an on-call pharmacist redistributes breaks them down and sends them to the unit for us to dispense."

"Who brings them to you in the nurses station?" Harry thought the whole operation seemed loose, without real structure. He'd worked under weird circumstances on travel nurse assignments, but this was the worst setup he'd ever seen.

Before Lena could answer, Eddie came banging on the window. "Hey! You gotta come quick. Dallas ain't breathing."

Harry turned to Lena. "Get the crash cart."

205

"We don't have one."

"What!"

"It was moved … to the Tunnel … in the ECT procedure room." Her words came out like a sputtering faucet.

Harry opened the door and ran down the hall. When he stepped into Dallas's room, Vinnie was already doing CPR.

"Good job, Vinnie. Stop a minute. Let me check him out"

"He was talking to me and he suddenly stopped and went limp."

Lena was standing in the doorway wringing her hands.

"Go get the defibrillator from the cart in ECT, Lena. Hurry!"

Harry was feeling Dallas's carotid, searching for a pulse. "Vinnie, take my phone. Call Gina. Tell her to come to your room! Now!

Harry felt a thready pulse, but Dallas wasn't breathing. Harry started counting, pressing down on Dallas's chest.

Gina stepped into the room, took one look, and turned. "I saw an ambu bag in one of the drawers in the nurses station. I'll be right back."

Harry kept up his compressions, then stooped and checked Dallas. Now, not even a thready pulse … and still no breathing. "Damn, where's Lena with that defibrillator?"

Gina came back with the ambu bag and mask. She positioned the mask over Dallas's mouth as Harry began compressions again. "Why the hell don't they at least have portable defibrillators on each floor?"

Lena came running back with the portable defib unit. Gina grabbed it, set it down next to Dallas, tore open his shirt, and slapped the pads on his chest. When everything was ready, she positioned the paddles. "Clear!"

It jolted the vet.

Harry immediately checked for a pulse. "Nothing."

"Is it ready … has it recharged yet?" Lena blurted.

Gina placed the paddles again. "Now! Clear!"

"Stop! I have a pulse," Harry called out.

Gina bagged Dallas and then he was breathing on his own.

Vinnie clutched Dallas's hand. "Man, you scared the life out of us."

Dallas gave him a weak smile, nodded. He took some deep breaths. "You know … guys … there was no light … at the end of the … fucking tunnel."

Chapter 42

Ziggy Jones had had it and figured Saturday might be a good time to clean out her things and leave her resignation letter on Delores's desk.

When she opened the drawer where she usually stored her purse, she was surprised to find an envelope taped to the side of the drawer. Her name was s scrawled across the front. She recognized Delores's handwriting.

She read the letter and was stunned, read it a second time.

Although almost everything Delores had written down were things she already knew, the information was fleshed out in great detail.

Ziggy pulled her personal thumb drive from her purse and attached it to the hospital computer. She didn't have to look around to see if anyone was watching her. She had ears like an elephant, could hear or sense any person in her vicinity. She figured she got that skill from her mother. She was the same way.

Not many visitors came through the Bone Point hospital doors. Most of the patients in the facility were virtually throwaways ... discarded people no one gave a damn about. Thinking about it made her very sad. She used to go home and cry about it, but once she decided to fight back, she stopped needing to cry.

Her husband told her not to make waves. "You're a black woman. You're only going to get in trouble." She stopped discussing it with him so he'd leave her alone. But she still kept up her files.

After using her password, she scanned Delores's letter and downloaded the contents.

Ziggy brought up what she called her kill list. These were the veterans who had died here but still remained in the computer as patients.

In the hospital computer files they lived on as ghostly images of the people who had floated through the doors of Bone Point. But few were discharged from this place. Most left feet first.

Oh, there were a few phony death certificates. They used those for the vets who were supposed to have autopsies for one reason or another. But it was all fake; the autopsies were never performed.

The fake paperwork was flawless.

But every single lie in Bone Point's file system was documented on her thumb drive. And next to each lie was the truth what had actually happened to each vet.

It didn't matter what her husband said. Morality is color blind. Her mother taught her that wrong is wrong.

Norman Glick and Delores Smiley only gave her relatively minor assignments. Her primary job was to gather background information on the patients next of kin, family members.

In this place, only a few of the vets listed any family at all. None gave the usual answers to the questions. But a while back, Ziggy had started notifying any listed friends, or designated advocates of a veteran's death, even though their files were active in the hospital.

None of the people she notified ever responded.

She reached into the coat closet and pulled out a large shopping bag filled with men's clothes. Some were used, a lot were from thrift stores, and a few were brand new.

She carried the bag to the elevator, pressed the five button. When she arrived, she walked across the floor to Donnie's sleeping area and set the bag down.

"Donnie? It's Ziggy."

In a few minutes Donnie came down out of his secluded corner. Just looking at him she could tell something was wrong.

"What's the matter, Donnie?" She held her arms open. Donnie let her hold him but he was shaking.

"Tell me. Let me help you."

Instead of speaking, he took her hand and together they walked back down the corridor. Soon Donnie started to slow his steps until he refused to move any farther.

"What is it?

Ziggy could remember the many times she came to see him and he was crying and moaning as though he wanted to die. One day he told her about his mother. She tried to help, searched through the files, but without a last name, she'd had no luck.

He took her to an old bathroom where he'd hidden something. He removed a black blanket and pointed.

She saw huge numbers of plastic drug containers piled up in the room. She couldn't imagine how many there were.

"Where did you get this?"

Donnie crouched down next to her, just shook his head.

"You know you can trust me." Ziggy gently rubbed his arm. "I would never do anything to hurt you."

Donnie looked at her and she could see he believed her. But he was still afraid.

She knew that according to the records, large amounts of drugs were still coming into the hospital, as though they still had sixty or more patients instead of the actual fifteen.

Delores had revealed in her letter to Ziggy that she and Norman were stock-piling patient drugs, but it didn't really make sense to Ziggy, until now.

She should have figured it out, but she always thought the administrators were stealing the vets' monthly benefits. Drugs never entered her mind.

"Who brought these up here?"

He shook his head.

"Was it Delores or Norman?"

He shook his head.

"Was it Thor or Eddie?"

Finally, he spoke. "Yes," he said in a little boy's voice.

"Did they put all of this here?"

"No." He stood, took her hand, and led her back across to the other end of the floor to an empty flatbed dolly.

"So they put it here and when they left, you moved it."

"Yes," he whispered.

"Why?"

"They're bad men. They hurt people."

Chapter 43

Saturday, late morning

Vinnie looked at Dallas, who was lying flat on his back. The man looked weak and vulnerable. A running IV bag hung on a pole close by his bed. Vinnie watched the drops fall into the port at a slow drip. His experience as a nurse tech at Ridgewood hospital told him Dallas was not only hydrating, but also had a vein open and ready if he got into trouble again.

"Will you stop looking at me like that?" Dallas said. "I'm going to be fine. If you ask me, I was only mostly dehydrated."

"You're a doctor now?"

Dallas didn't come back with the usual smart-ass remark. Instead, he said, "You sound like your brother-in-law."

"Yeah, he told me you refused an ambulance ride to the nearest hospital."

"I'm not the one to worry about. "You've got to get out of here, man. They're going to kill you."

"I'm not that easy to kill, and I can't leave until I find out what happened to my buddy, Guy."

"Oh, for shit's sake, get a life will you? In case you haven't figured it out, they killed Guy so they could steal his drugs. That's why they killed most of them."

"You just want me to run. I don't believe you."

"Don't you get it? The people here are not going to die a natural death. Think of Rick Bell."

"You're just saying whatever pops into your head. I still don't believe it."

"Take a look around. Most of the vets are going to be taken out feet first even though they're *physically* okay.*"

"Says the guy who can barely lift an arm."

"Look, man, if you wait long enough, lots of them are going to die a premature death anyway. Drugs, alcohol, dope, depression. All killers. Like it or not, in a short time they'll all be dead, whether it's at someone else's hand or not."

"So who's stealing their drugs … and why?"

"Vinnie, Vinnie! I don't believe you're from the Bronx. Who else but Norman, the administrator. He's selling them and making a huge wad of cash."

"But Guy☐"

"Cut it out, will you? Guy was crazy. It didn't matter where he went down. It was all over for him from the first moment he stepped onto Afghanistan soil. And not only him. A downhill ride for you and for me."

"But☐"

"Just get out of here. Go home to your fiancée, stick with your counselor and your group, and have the best life you can. It's the only way to win."

"Man, you're depressing me. You're talking like it's all over for you."

"Face it. I'm not getting out of here alive."

Gina slipped into the room. She was dressed in jeans and a sweatshirt. Vinnie thought she looked like a pregnant kid who was going to catch 4hell from her parents for having gotten knocked up.

"Hi, you two. How's our miracle patient doing?"

Now that Harry was here, Vinnie could see his sister was more like her old feisty self again.

"Hey, Dallas," Gina said, "I see you have a little more color in your face. You know you scared the hell out of us."

"I've been trying to convince your brother☐"

"Hey, lower your voice. No one is supposed to know Vinnie is my brother."

That brought more color to Dallas's face. "Sorry. Won't happen again." He looked at the dripping solution in the IV port. "You need to get your Vinnie out of here. Like, now."

214

"You hear him, Vinnie? Let's go get Harry and go home."

Vinnie shook his head slowly back and forth. "How can we just walk out of here if what Dallas says is true?"

Gina stared at her brother, obviously puzzled.

"He says they're murdering vets to steal their drugs and sell them."

She stood with her hands on her hips thinking. Finally she said, "Ah-huh. Now that makes sense. That's why there are so many vets still active-listed when there are really only fifteen actual patients. They're keeping their drugs."

Dallas nodded. "The VA is one crazy, bureaucratic madhouse. Even with computers they're way behind on everything. And most of their computers are not state-of-the-art." He laughed. "It can take them months on end to effectively catch up … with anything."

"Listen to the man, Vinnie," Gina said. "Let's get Harry and walk out the front door together. We can go to the authorities afterward."

"Oh, no, you don't. Maybe I couldn't save Guy, but I'm not leaving Dallas behind."

* * *

Norman was stressed, more stressed than at any time he could ever remember. He tapped his finger on the desk in a frantic rhythm and listened intently as he mentally tried to get Kevin to pick up his phone. It occurred to him that he didn't even know Kevin-the-ghoul's last name.

"Shit!" He disconnected and punched in the number again. He could feel the bile building at the back of his throat. It rang again. And again.

"Pick up, damn it!"

The administrator had been trying to get Kevin since yesterday without any luck.

Come on! Come on!

Finally, Kevin's voice was at the other end. Norman wanted to scream his head off.

"Yeah?"

"Where have you been, Kev?" He was biting his lip to keep from yelling at the dolt. "I've been trying to get you since yesterday. Weren't you supposed to come by and take care of those stiffs for me?"

"So?"

"Well. What happened?"

"I got busy. Forgot. Besides, it's Saturday. Don't usually do work on weekends."

Norman reined in his temper. He was in no position to mess this up. He was screwed if Kevin didn't come and do the job.

"Will you do it today?"

"Can't get the boat until after three."

"Fine. Why don't you pick up the stiffs now and do the rest later when you have the boat."

Silence.

"Kevin?"

"Want more money. Not worth it anymore."

Norman wanted to pull his hair out. He'd been dealing with the man for three years, paying one thousand dollars cash per body.

"How much do you want?"

"Double. Two grand each. Cash, like before."

Norman did some quick calculations: He was going to have to get rid of all fifteen of the remaining patients. He probably could make it work, if he took the cash out of the discretionary fund to pay Kevin. It was worth it just to get it done.

Only two months left to cover the "transfer" of those last fifteen patients. He was counting on the bureaucratic morass to lose them.

"Okay. You've got a deal," Norman said. "Will you come now?"

"Be there in half an hour."

Chapter 44

Stepping outside from Vinnie's and Dallas' room, Gina said to Harry, "You need to see what I saw in the Tunnel. I think they're killing the vets and stealing their drugs."

"I'd rather get out of this place. It's toxic. I can feel it closing in on all of us. Let's get Vinnie and go." Harry had that determined look on his face.

"I know my brother. He's not going anywhere without Dallas. Besides, I can't unsee what's being done here."

"First it's Guy, now it's Dallas?"

"Look, Harry, maybe he couldn't save Guy, but he does have a chance to save Dallas. We've got to help make things right for my brother."

He reached over and kissed her cheek "There're a million reasons why I love you. This is one of them." He took her hand. "You really think they're killing the vets for their drugs?"

"Do you find that so hard to believe?"

"Okay, show me what you saw." He squeezed her hand. "We can't keep standing around here off duty. Especially together. Let's go."

They headed for the staircase.

When they reached the bottom floor, Gina started toward the room where the bodies were.

A giant of a man, at least six and a half feet, dressed in grubby jeans and a rain jacket was wheeling out a sheet-covered body from the room.

"What are you doing?" Gina glanced inside. The other two bodies were gone.

"I was told to pick up these stiffs."

217

Gina watched the man's hands clutch the sides of the table. He wouldn't look her in the eye.

Harry said, "Who told you?"

The man remained silent.

"Do you have papers that authorize you to take these bodies away?" Gina asked.

Harry moved up to the gurney. "You heard her. Where are the papers?"

Without a word, the man shoved Harry so hard he crashed against the corridor wall. Dazed, he slid to the floor. The man was on him and started beating him.

Gina rushed over. "Stop it! Get off of him!"

The man shrugged her off. But she grabbed handfuls of his hair with both hands and yanked hard, harder. He turned from Harry and flung her away, grabbed the gurney and headed down the corridor.

She landed on her rump but was up right away. "Harry, Harry, are you all right?" She hugged him to her before examining his head. No lacerations or external bleeding. He was clutching at his gut.

In a moment, he stood. "Where's that bastard?"

"Are you okay?" Gina asked.

"Where is he? How did he get out of here?"

Gina pointed.

They ran down the corridor to a set of exit doors. They flung them open as the man was getting into a white panel truck. He drove away.

"Did you get the license plate number?" Harry shouted.

"No, it was covered in mud." Gina was clutching her belly.

Harry grabbed her shoulders. "Did he hurt you? Are you having any pain? Tell me!"

She shook her head. Tears ran down her cheeks.

"Gina, talk to me. What's the matter?"

"I'm all right. But I … I was so scared … scared he might kill you."

"Doll, I'm right here and I'm okay."

"I know, but what if he had? I can't stand it … can't stand the thought of losing you."

He took her in his arms and rocked her, kissed her tears away.

Finally, she smiled at him. "Damn hormones."

* * *

Thor was walking on air. He and Eddie were even getting along without their usual bickering. Thor couldn't believe how the morning had flown by. After bringing up the lunch trays, they decided to check their stash of drugs.

"Hey, Tony, how about covering for us? We need to do something."

Tony, the handyman, was a pudgy twenty-five year old who'd been out sick for the last four days. In fact, Tony was out sick a lot of the time. "No way! I'm no sucker for the two of you.

Thor said, "If you don't do it I'll beat the shit out of you. … and you know I will."

"Okay. Just don't make it too long." Tony immediately started picking at a pimple on his chin, probably in aggravation.

When Thor and Eddie reached the fifth floor, they raced down the hall to where they'd left the dolly.

Thor was the first to speak. "What the □"

Eddie could barely get the words out. "It's gone. Everything is gone."

"No!" Thor yelled. "No, no, no!"

Chapter 45

Saturday, Noon

Gina was furious that they couldn't stop that ghoul from stealing the three veterans' bodies.

Would have been messy if we caught up to him. He was as big as a battleship.

"Are you okay?" Harry said.

"Harry, stop it! Stop asking me that! I'm tired of all of us worrying about the worst-case scenario for this pregnancy. We both worry, worry, worry. I swear, it's going to turn me into a hypochondriac."

He took her into his arms and nuzzled her neck. "It's only four more months, doll. After that we can worry about the baby instead."

Gina started laughing. "Harry Lucke, you're going to be such a great dad."

"We'll be great together."

They started down the Tunnel corridor again, holding each other's hand.

"That big *schlub* wasn't working for a funeral home." Gina hunched her shoulders. "It gets really creepy when I wonder what he's going to do with the bodies."

"Good question." Harry gently fingered the bump that had blossomed on his head. "I think you're right about what's going on here."

"Dallas was the one to spill the beans. He said those men didn't just die, they were murdered."

"You say you looked at the bodies?"

"Well, I was spooked out. I didn't really study them. But they didn't look hurt or beaten ... they just looked ... dead."

221

As they passed the storage rooms, Harry stopped. "Look, the security boxes have been ripped apart."

Gina touched the broken wood, saw the wires had been cut in both security boxes.

Harry pulled on one door, Gina pulled on the other.

"Whatever was in here is gone," Harry said.

"Same here." She no sooner said it when she saw some pills scattered on the floor. She picked one up. "Looks like Vicodin," she said.

They looked at each other.

"Drugs. That's exactly what was in these rooms," Gina said.

"To think I had my doubts." Harry said.

Gina grabbed his hand. "Let's get out of here. I've had enough of this creepy Tunnel and this creepy hospital."

* * *

Where was that loser, Norman? Manky hadn't heard a word from the *putz*.

Maybe I'm losing it. A jerk like that should have been scared shitless; instead he's making me look weak.

Manky picked up his cell phone and tapped the number for Norman.

That ass better pick up.

But it rang and rang, forcing Manky to call him again and again.

Nothing.

The last time Manky left a message:

"Listen, you piece of shit. You better call me in the next five minutes or you're dead. Get it?"

Manky kept checking his watch. When there were thirty seconds left, Norman buzzed Manky's phone.

He tapped onto the line. "And why aren't you here? I told you I wanted the rest of my product today."

"Don't take it the wrong way."

"And how should I take it?"

"Just a lot of hospital business."

"Well, asshole, I have business, too. When are you bringing me my product?"

There was a long pause.

"I'm waiting. And I don't like to wait."

"You almost killed Dallas. He's my, or was my go between. I don't have anyone else who can deliver."

"What's the matter with your ass hauling it here? Get in the car, start it, and bring me my goods."

"I don't do deliveries."

"But you do money, don't you?"

Norman seemed to think that was pretty fucking funny. "That's the name of the game ... isn't it?"

Manky didn't like his hotshot attitude. His grandfather would have not pegged Norman as a decent man. Yeah, it was true, Manky had made a bundle since they started doing business together, but he could see that whole deal was coming to an end, even sooner than he'd thought just an hour ago.

"I don't fucking care who brings it. You get me my product or you're dead."

Norman was silent.

So, you thought Dallas looked bad? Think about this: I like Dallas, so he got off easy. You, I don't like, so there is no easy way out. Got it?"

With that, he clicked off.

* * *

The elevator chugged slowly down to the Tunnel, a stark contrast to Norman's inner turmoil. He tried to focus, but his head was racing, spinning. He could picture himself standing on the top of a twenty-story building getting ready to jump.

Damn it. When had his life turned to shit?

But he knew exactly when.

* * *

Norman's uniform was itching, but the major conducting the class would not appreciate his scratching himself, especially since he was sitting in the front row of the classroom.

The itching made it hard to concentrate, but the subject the nature of conflict and how military forces are developed and deployed was one of his favorites in the ROTC program. If he was lucky, he would someday not only be an officer in the Air Force, he would be a pilot. That was his goal.

At the end of the class, the major handed him a note:

Appear at 1600 hours at Commander Muller's office.

At the appointed time, Norman walked up to the sergeant sitting outside the commander's office.

"Norman Glick?" the sergeant asked before he could say anything.

"Yes, Sergeant."

The NCO picked up the phone and advised the commander that Norman Glick was there.

Norman glanced at his watch. Five minutes late.

Damn it! Should never have changed majors.

The sergeant nodded for him to go into the office. As soon as he entered, the NCO closed the door. Norman approached the desk, saluted the commander. His gut was clenched in fear, even though he knew what was coming. Why hadn't he been smart enough to avoid this?

He stood at attention.

There were no preliminaries. "You know why you're here?"

"Yes, sir."

"You will no longer be a part of this fine group of future officers." He sarcastically added, "But I think the Air Force will survive without the likes of you. Now get out of my sight."

As he walked away, the sergeant was smirking.

But the realization, the pain of knowing he was never going to be a pilot, all because he changed majors from aeronautical engineering to BusEd, against his better judgment. It was making him sick.

He had his parents to thank for that.

They'd threatened to cut him off financially unless he became a business major. Now he wouldn't finish college in four years, reason enough to drop him from the ROTC program. It stabbed him through the heart.

He'd hated the military ever since.

The only thing that ever hurt him more was the death of his dog Topper.

* * *

The elevator finally arrived at the Tunnel. He stepped out and stood there for a moment. For the first time in years, he felt a wave of despair wash over him.

Baloney. That was then, this is now.

After seeing what that nut job Manky did to Dallas, maybe it was time to cut his losses and disappear.

Get out of here and run. Sell the whole kit and caboodle to Manky at some cut-rate price and get lost before the man decided to kill him.

Chapter 46

Norman was thunderstruck.

He stood in front of the two storage rooms where his stash of drugs had been stored. He fingered the ruined security boxes.

Everything was gone. His chest was exploding; he could barely breathe. He stepped inside as though that would make everything magically reappear. That maybe this was just some kind of crazy, eyes-open hallucination.

But he couldn't be that lucky.

He leaned against the storage room wall with all of his weight to keep from collapsing. Then he slid down to the floor. His bottom hit so hard, it jolted everything in his body.

What am I going to do?

He kept rubbing his head as though he could help his brain spit out an answer.

Maybe he could pay Manky the street value of the stash?

He quickly calculated his cash-in-hand status. Maybe, just maybe, he could put together a million. With all his investments, he was worth at least five million. But it would take time to turn any of that into liquid cash.

The missing stash had probably been worth one to two million. Although it wasn't like Manky to ever let slip what he raked in, it still had to be in the millions.

Norman began to feel better. He could take a deep breath again.

After all, what did Manky really want?

Product.

Product always equaled money.

The edge of smile was worked its way to his lips.

Maybe, just maybe I can pull this off.

227

* * *

Norman's bravado disappeared as he clutched the phone, waiting for Manky to answer.

After the fourth ring, the phone was picked up. Silence.

"Manky?"

"I have nothing to say to you. I want my product and I want it now!"

Norman's entire body was shaking. "Listen, I have a proposition that I think you'll find agreeable."

"We already have a contract. I'm waiting for you to stand behind your word."

Norman waited, trying to compose a strategy that the drug dealer might go for. "Why don't I pay you one million dollars in place of the delivery."

The silence was so profound, they might as well have been in outer space □a place where there's only silence.

"Manky? Are you there?"

"I didn't think you were this stupid."

"You don't understand," Norman said. The words flew from his mouth before he could think about it. "My whole stock has been stolen. I mean, there's nothing left."

"I'm supposed to believe that?"

"It's the truth. I swear."

"No!"

"I don't understand."

"Let me make it perfectly clear. The truth? You sold your product to my competitors and have left me shortchanged and vulnerable. That's the truth."

"No, no! That's why I'm willing to fork over a million to you. Even two million if we can be even again."

"Two million? To you this is a lot of money … to me, it's nothing."

"I thought it was a fair amount."

"It's not all about money, you idiot. It's about trust between me and my buyers, who in turn are distributors that have their own distributors. And on and on."

"I see," Norman said.

"I don't think you do." Manky cleared his throat. "The whole chain starts to dry up when obligations are not met. But why am I bothering to explain this to a dead man?"

"What can I do? Someone stole my whole stash."

"I don't believe you."

"What can I do to make this right?"

There was no response.

"Did you hear me, Manky?"

Silence.

"What can I do to fix this?"

The line went dead.

* * *

Vinnie stood at the side of Dallas's bed. He opened his hand. "See here, man."

"What've you got there, big guy? Hey, looks like a shitload of pills."

"I've finally got that Lena nurse snookered. She thinks she can trust me now. These critters stayed right under my tongue when I gulped the water."

"Total clarity. How does it feel?"

"Kind of strange. For the first time I'm beginning to see what an idiot I was to sign into this hell hole." Vinnie shook his head slowly. "I really loved Guy. He was the only one I had left of our unit. But nothing is going to bring back my buddy."

"Now you're getting some sense in that stubborn head of yours."

Dallas still looked like he was in terrible shape. Vinnie reached over and reset his pillow to make him more comfortable.

"You're soft, Vinnie. Nothing but a mother hen."

"You ought to try working with patients yourself one day. You not only learn a lot, but it makes you feel a whole lot better about yourself."

"I think you're right. At least, it's about time I started thinking of doing something solid to earn a living again. It was hard to hold down a job living on the streets. I'd almost given up even trying when I got this gig."

"What exactly did you do for the administrator?"

"Let's just say I'm a go-between, or I used to be, for some of his transactions."

"I'll bet you can get a job at Ridgewood Hospital in San Francisco. That's where I work. That's how I met my fiancée. Well, she's also a friend of Gina's."

"It's a cozy little gig you've got with your sister, Harry, and your fiancée."

"Hey, it's all about family. Don't knock it 'til you've tried it."

Dallas had a far-away look in his eyes. "I'd give anything to be with my family again."

"Well, do it, man."

"No. I kinda ruined that a long time ago."

Vinnie touched his shoulder. "Are you sure?"

"I let them down, Vinnie. It's hard to face them."

"Maybe they don't feel that way … and even if they did, don't you think they can forgive you?"

"What I do know? It's hard to forgive myself."

The door to the room was shoved open.

"Hey, you two." Thor and Eddie came rushing in together. Vinnie looked at their faces and knew they were about to be thrown into the first circle of hell.

As usual, Thor was the bigmouth. "Where is it?"

Vinnie stood in front of Dallas. "Where's what?"

Thor shoved Vinnie to the side. He jabbed a finger into Dallas's shoulder. "You know what I'm talking about."

"I haven't got a clue," Dallas said.

Eddie jumped in. "You know, the stuff in the storage rooms in the Tunnel."

Dallas managed to sit up. "What room?" He glared at Thor. "You two must have been smoking too much of that weed you're always carrying around."

"Get the gurney, Eddie. Let's take this piece of shit to the ECT room. Maybe a little electrical juice will clear his head."

"Or fry his brain forever." Eddie threw the words over his shoulder as he went for a gurney.

"Leave him alone, you asshole," Vinnie shouted, getting between Thor and Dallas.

Thor punched Vinnie's face so hard, he flew into the wall.

"You!" Thor pointed at Vinnie. "You're coming down with your buddy.

Dallas looked at Thor with pure hatred. "Leave him alone. He doesn't know anything."

Thor smiled at Dallas. "But you sure as shit do."

Bette Golden Lamb & J. J. Lamb

232

Chapter 47

Saturday, Noon

Allison York was frustrated by a lack of progress in the Bone Point case. She'd been working on it this for four months and could not validate the claims Ziggy Jones made.

The IG agent had gone over it again and again, but it didn't amount to a solid case. If there was hard evidence it would have to come from Ziggy, who was a very reluctant informant.

She'd called Isaac at home and asked if he would come in and help her.

"You can see what I'm up against," she said. "It's a long way from proving criminal intent. And it's all over once they close down that place."

Isaac studied the computer screen.

"I need to check out the actual workings of Bone Point, get into their computers," Allison said. "With what I have so far, I'm not going anywhere. I need hard evidence or the people who run that hospital will just move on to another failing vet hospital, and start over again."

"It's seems to be a pattern," Isaac said.

"It's freakin' awful. The hospitals get dinged for poor performance and people like Norman Glick move in to improve their services, but all these new administrators really do is cut back on services to improve their stats. In the end, it guarantees failure."

"Yeah," Isaac said. "This is a hard one."

"Ziggy said there was some talk of drug involvement. I tried calling a friend at the DEA but it's the same old story not enough to go on to even grab their interest."

Isaac turned away from the computer. "This Ziggy Jones. She's the real thing?"

"Oh, I don't doubt that. That woman has been sticking her neck out gathering information. She's scared to death. Afraid of being caught. Afraid of even meeting with me."

"Would they hurt her? This sounds like more of a white collar crime."

"Her reports talk about two ex-cons who are working there as orderlies. They're supposedly abusive to the patients and she doesn't think they would hesitate to kill her if the administrator, Norman Glick, ordered it."

Isaac leaned over the desk and looked into her eyes. "Let's move away from murder for a sec. Why don't I stay over at your place tonight?"

She couldn't believe she was actually blushing. "I don't know if I'm ready for that, Isaac. I mean you staying over."

"We're both ready … and we both know it."

She gave him a fleeting smile. "Let's talk about it later. Right now I'm worried about Ziggy Jones and finding a way to nab these rats at Bone Point."

He reached across the desk and squeezed her hand. "Don't worry. We'll nail them."

"Not if I can't get some hard evidence. I'm worried. Ziggy's not a pro. What if she gets caught?"

"She should have brought you some hard copy, a little at a time."

Allison leaned back into her seat. "Ziggy is basically a loyal employee. It's hard for that type of person to just strike out against someone who trusts her.

I asked her to bring me anything she'd gathered. But I knew if I pushed too hard, I could lose her altogether. I can't take a chance on losing her. She's all I have."

Chapter 48

Saturday, 1:00 pm

Ziggy watched Delores stomp into her office and slam the door.

I knew I shouldn't have come in today, should have waited until tomorrow.

"Ziggy!" Norman yelled from his office.

She reluctantly left her desk and went to see what he wanted.

"I'm only here to pick up a few things, not to work. You've had me in here too many weekends this month as it is."

"I don't give a damn why you're here, just go get Delores and bring her to my office." His face was flushed, his eyes wild.

"I don't think that's my job," Ziggy said.

The administrator stood and started around his desk, hands balled into fists. "I'm making it your job. Go get her!"

Ziggy took a step back, shaking, certain he was about to strike her. She turned and headed toward Delores's office.

She knocked and said through the closed door, "Delores, he wants to see you."

"Tell him to forget it," Delores yelled. "I'm not involved with any of this anymore."

Ziggy tapped on the door and went in.

Delores's face was blanched, her eyes unfocused.

"I found your envelope," Ziggy said softly. "What do you want me to do with it? It's very incriminating for you."

"It doesn't make any difference. I'm through ... through with all of it. It's time to make the veterans our first concern. That's why we were sent here in the first place."

"But is there something specific you want me to do?"

"Right now, all I want is for you to go tell that asshole down the hall that I'm not coming to his office, now or ever again."

When Ziggy relayed the gist of the message, Norman snarled at her like a trapped animal.

Her stomach was in knots. The administrator had been screaming at her for days. Friday he'd given her long handwritten list of names and telephone numbers he wanted her to reach out to. She'd never heard of any of these people and she was sure they had nothing to do with the hospital.

Not one of them would take his call.

The last phone number was for a private air service.

Her panic surged until she felt like she was going to explode. The worst part was seeing that poor man Dallas beaten up, stuck in a wheelchair, and forced to go to Norman's office.

Dallas had looked half-dead already. Ziggy had been the only person to help him back to his room and into bed. No one seemed to care.

Is that what's going to happen to me?

Beaten to a pulp?

Norman was again screaming for her to get into his office.

Her head was hot. Everything was raw and explosive all around her.

Her gut was telling her to get out.

Get out right *now*, before it was too late.

Ziggy gathered up her flash drive, collected all of the printed computer data records she'd kept hidden in her coat closet, stuffed everything into two large manila envelopes. She snatched up her raincoat, slipped into it, and headed for the hospital exit.

She heard Norman yell out at her.

"Ziggy, come back here. Where are you going?" He started running toward her.

"Family emergency," she yelled back. "Have to leave for awhile." She turned her back on him and hurried out the door, heading for the parking area.

Heavy rain drenched her the moment she stepped outside. She thrust the envelopes under her coat, close to her chest, and ran for her Malibu.

236

Norman sprinted out into the rain and chased after her.

She pulled the keys from her pocket, opened the door, and dove into the car.

Norman loomed closer and closer.

Please start! Please start!

When he was only ten feet away, close enough for her to see his hands drawn into fists and his eyes shooting bolts of rage, the car came alive.

She jammed the car into reverse, stomped on the accelerator. When she was clear of the parking space, she swung around to the right, grazing Norman before she roared out of the parking lot.

When she finally dared to look in the rearview mirror, he was only a black dot.

Ziggy used the special number Agent York had given her for emergencies. Looked back again to see if she was being followed, then called.

"It's me, Ziggy."

"Are you all right? You sound awful."

"I think I've got all the information you asked for. I hope so because I can't go back."

"Where are you?"

"On my way to San Francisco," Ziggy shouted into her cell. "I've never been so scared in my life. I'll feel better when you have all the stuff I've collected."

"Come straight to my office; I'm already here."

* * *

The IG agent was waiting for Ziggy in the agency's parking lot. Allison watched the woman sit with her hands on the wheel for several moments before she lifted herself from the car. She was clutching large manila envelopes to her chest, but her face was stretched into a wide smile.

The rain had stopped; the sun was out and shining.

Allison walked out to meet her.

Chapter 49

Donnie stood by the fifth-floor window looking out. Everything looked a soothing gray. The rain was coming down so hard it was like long metal nails being pounded into the ground.

He liked the world when the sky opened up and water rushed to the ground. It always made him feel quiet and calm. It started him thinking about his mother again. When he felt peaceful like this, he could see her features much more clearly in his mind. She liked to sing to him when it was raining.

He came out of his trance when he saw Ziggy running. A man was chasing her. The muscles in Donnie's neck tensed until his head hurt.

The man was getting closer, closer, until it looked like he might catch her. But then she got into a car and drove away.

Donnie relaxed.

The man just stood there, didn't seem to notice the rain making him all wet. Soon he turned around.

Donnie moved away from the window and walked back to the bathroom where he'd stored all drugs. They were still hidden and safe.

Ziggy told him not to touch them. He was supposed to wait for her. She said she would come back to take care of it.

* * *

Norman was puzzled. Why did Ziggy run from him? Why would she run?

And why like an idiot, did I take after her?

True, he'd been on a rampage all day. Was that the reason she was suddenly afraid of him. Or was there more to it?

And with all his problems, he'd been forced to go upstairs and take a shower again, change his clothes, and all because he'd chased after her in the rain.

Stupid fool.

Back in his office, Norman looked around at his hole-in-the-wall space. As he studied the room, he realized it had the atmosphere of a low-level office worker. No pictures on the wall, a simple ugly desk. There weren't even any framed images of loved ones facing him to feel warm and fuzzy about. He might as well have been in a rat in a maze.

The image bothered him.

He got up and walked the short length of the room, then returned to his seat. He knew he was drifting when he should have been highly focused. But his mind kept wandering.

At this point in his life, shouldn't he be asking the big questions:

Why was he here?

What was life all about?

Who did he love?

What was most important to him?

He didn't need to ask those silly questions. He already knew the answers. It was all so simple. Why complicate it?

He wanted money. And more of it. There was *never* enough.

Isn't that what everybody wanted?

The women in is life were few and unimportant. His parents? The last time he'd seen them or his brother was ten years ago. As far as he was concerned, Mom and Dad had ruined his life a long time ago when he adapted to the same reason for living that they had.

I've got to stop this introspective crap. It's useless inertia ... like being caught in a pool of quicksand.

Who stole my drugs, damn it?

Why did Ziggy run? Did she run because she had something to do with the disappearance of the drugs?

Or was it those two orderlies who were so involved in my affairs?

No, all they cared about was staying out of prison. Or as Delores said, beating up the vets. They'd never have enough brains to bring this off.

For the briefest of moments he thought about the vets.

Norman always thought he'd given these broken people a graceful way out. They served a better purpose now, even had a better life, existing as ghosts in a computer. Ghosts that allowed him to make more and more money.

Do I regret any of it?

From what hole in my brain did that crawl out from?

Fuck them! And fuck all the peons in the world who weren't smart enough to use the system to their advantage.

Yes. Fuck them.

Now get on with it. Figure it out. Act!

First and foremost he needed to stall Manky so he could get away. If only he could try one more time to talk Delores into going to Manky and explaining what happened, it would buy him time. When that beast came, he'd be long gone.

* * *

Delores was confused, didn't know what to do. She knew she should be checking on the patients' unit to make sure everything was running smoothly. But it was hard to think.

Someone tapped on her door.

Norman came in, a hand held up in peace.

"What do you want?"

He sat down in her office chair. She could see he was trying to be calm, even pleasant.

"Delores, we've been working together for so many years. Good productive years. We've both made money. We can continue to do that."

"Again, what do you want, Norman?" What *she* wanted was to run away.

"Please, please go to Manky. Explain why there's a delay."
He just sat there, color draining from his face.

"You keep skirting the question. Why is there a delay? Just give the criminal what he wants. It's simple. All he wants is what you've been giving him for years."

Norman carefully folded one hand over another in his lap. "Someone broke in and stole our whole supply of stashed drugs."

Totally stunned, Delores said, "And you want me to go and tell him that?"

"It's your neck, too. I think he'll be a lot easier on a woman than a man."

"Get out of here, you miserable coward!"

* * *

Delores was right. He needed to get out of here.

Now!

Back in his office, he snatched up the phone.

"Remember me? I spoke to you about a ride to Nogales."

"Yes, of course."

"Three o'clock?"

"That will work out very well, sir."

"See you then."

"Sir?"

"Yes?"

"Don't forget your passport."

Chapter 50

It was a fucked-up two days for Manky.

Although he was at the top of the heap, he had obligations that had to be met. He had to get the goods to his people.

Now!

He hadn't been challenged for years, but he knew that either he gave his distributors what was promised or he would go down, and it would be a ruthless, brutal slide to hell.

That's how *he* would handle weakness.

Better than anyone, he knew how easy it was to lose fancy digs — his homes in Belarus, Mexico City, London, and here in Marin County.

But his power?

Death was nothing. Power was everything. The next in line would snuff him out without a second thought.

What would you do, Grandfather? What would you do?

Manky thought for a moment.

He would just have to lose the money. They would have to break into one of their many backup storage units and replace what Norman Glick didn't deliver.

The distributors were already suspicious, and if Manky didn't deliver today, they would get their goods from the Caldero Seven, a huge family-owned franchise that had been nipping at his ass, trying to unseat him for years. There'd been peace between them for a long time, but if they thought they could put Manky down …
well … there'd be no *discussion* about it.

He had to straighten this out. Now!

Manky was shaken. He'd become soft, and sloppy. He should have moved on Norman two days ago, but he thought Dallas would be warning enough for some little *putz* like Norman.

243

Grandpa always said: Don't underestimate your enemy.

Norman had become his enemy and Manky had underestimated him.

* * *

Manky and Hernando finished their plan, agreed that Norman would be brought in as an example of what would happen if people didn't live up to their obligations. At least Norman was a lone operator; there would be no family to take down. No future war.

"What about Dallas?" Hernando asked.

Manky thought a moment. "Dallas is just a delivery boy and he's had his warning. Grandfather would have called him a decent man who tried to serve Norman well. He's been punished enough for choosing the wrong person to serve."

"A shot to the head would be fast."

"If you have to, do it."

* * *

Norman Glick looked around his bedroom. His mind was jumping; he couldn't focus on any one thing except the time. He had to get to that plane by three o'clock.

Calm down. That airstrip's only fifteen miles away. You're acting like an idiot. Everything is taken care of. Just get to the plane and you're home free.

He took a few deep breaths and reached up to the top shelf of his closet for his tote bag. He threw it on the bed and filled it with underwear, a shirt, jeans, sneakers, and zipped it up.

He patted his pockets: passport, wallet filled with enough cash until he could get to an ATM.

One last look around and he was out the door.

"Can't wait for the damn elevator," he mumbled as he took to the stairs and raced down the four floors to the lobby.

Adrenalin pounded through him as he hurried through the exit and was out in the rain. He sprinted to his Mercedes as though someone were riding his heels. He tossed the bag into the trunk and hurried into the driver's seat.

When he drove out onto the main road, he let out a long sigh.

Made it! I'm free.

It would take a half-hour at the very most to get to the private airstrip and then he was off to Mexico. He had no idea where he was going after that. But he'd work that out later.

He was starting to relax when a head popped up from the backseat.

"*Ola, Señor.*"

Startled, he stared in the rearview mirror. "Hernando! What the fuck are doing in my car?"

"Manky sent me."

His body suddenly went slack … he wet his pants.

"I was going to call him later."

"Sure you were. But Manky thinks the time for conversation is over. Was over two days ago." Hernando put a heavy hand on his shoulder.

Norman wanted to plead, to beg, but he just kept staring at Hernando in the rearview mirror.

"Don't look at me, man. Keep driving! I'll give you all the directions you need."

Norman yelled out, "I'll give you money! Anything you want. Please let me go, Hernando. Please!"

"Money? You think you can buy your life with money?"

"Please let me go. Please."

"Manky asked me to tell you that no matter what you say, it's too late for you. Too late for a person like you to become a decent man."

Chapter 51

"Eddie, for shit's sake, move that gurney and get Dallas in here."

Dallas lifted his head, could see Thor pushing Vinnie ahead of him into the ECT room. He kept beating on Vinnie's back, making him stumble.

"What am I, your slave, or something?" Eddie said.

Thor ignored him and threw Vinnie onto the ECT table. He was fighting, punching wildly at Thor up until the orderly got his wrists into the restraints.

Thor punched Vinnie on the side of the head until he was dazed. "Dallas, you're gonna talk or your roommate is going to die. Get it?"

Dallas twisted, tried to move. He knew he had to help Vinnie.

"Stop!" Dallas shouted. His arms were like weights he couldn't lift. "Leave him alone. He doesn't know anything about the drugs."

Thor said, "You see, Dallas, you're already talking."

After Vinnie's ankles were restrained, Thor thrust his face right into Vinnie's and shook his shoulders.

"I got you now. You're mine." Thor slipped around to the head of the table and switched on the electric convulsive power unit.

Eddie moved next to Thor to watch. "This is a kick. I've always wanted to run this thing."

"Yeah, it's cool watching those psychos juice up."

* * *

Gina and Harry were on their way to the elevator. It was getting close to time for Harry to sign onto his shift. "You're going home, Gina."

247

Bette Golden Lamb & J. J. Lamb

"I am not!"

Harry cradled her hands in his. "You don't get it, do you?"

"I do, Harry. I really do."

He held her at arm's length. "You think it's all about the baby, don't you? What you're not seeing is that's just a part of it."

"What am I missing?"

"We've been on a rough journey together, doll. Your ex tried to kill you again and again. And your constant running away from me, not wanting to trust anybody ... until finally we married." He leaned over and kissed her neck. "I'm just so happy that now we have ... us!"

She smiled. "Me, too."

"It isn't only about the baby. I'd love you forever ... baby or no baby."

"I know, Harry, but—"

"I can't take a chance on losing you. You have to leave now."

"Okay, we'll both go. Let's get Vinnie ... even if we have to carry him out of here."

Harry pushed the number two button, but the elevator bypassed the second floor, and the first.

"What's with this ancient piece of junk?" Harry said.

The door finally clunked open at the Tunnel level.

"Not here," Gina said. "I've had my fill of this damn place."

Harry started to push two again, but Gina grabbed his hand.

"Did you hear that?"

"Hear what?"

"Shush! Listen!"

* * *

"Okay, man." Eddie said. "Gonna strap these things to your head. Good and tight. Oops, almost forgot that sticky stuff. There you go. "

"You're going to pay for this!" Vinnie shouted.

* * *

"It's my brother!" Gina said, moving toward the voices.

248

Harry grabbed her arm and whispered, "No! Wait! Listen!"

* * *

"You piece of shit, leave Vinnie alone," another voice said. "You don't want him. It's me you want."

* * *

"Is that Dallas?" Gina whispered.

Harry nodded.

* * *

"What did you do with our drugs?" Thor demanded.

"Does it look like I could move your drugs?"

* * *

Gina jerked out of Harry's grasp and ran to the procedure room.

Thor was leaning over Vinnie on the ECT table, yelling into his face:

"And *you're* not getting the juice that keeps your muscles from blowing up, little man."

He grabbed Vinnie's face, squeezed his mouth open, exposing his teeth. "Those pretty grinders? They're gonna be smashed to pieces."

"Let him go!" Gina started toward Thor, but Harry moved in and pushed her behind him.

"What the□"

"Is this your idea of fun?" Harry said to Thor across the ECT table.

"As a matter of fact, it is." Thor raised his hands and cracked his knuckles.

"Well, find something else to play with." Harry quickly undid a wrist restraint. Vinnie's hand was free.

"No way," Thor yelled.

Harry snatched his stethoscope from around his neck, snapped the end of it at Thor's face, catching him between the eyes.

Thor staggered, covered his face. "Turn on the juice," he barked at Eddie.

Eddie seemed stunned, stepped next to the gurney.

"Did you hear me? Turn it on!"

Thor lashed out, wrapped an arm around Harry's neck and squeezed tighter and tighter.

Dallas reached up and slapped Eddie's face.

"You son of a bitch!" Eddie raised a fist to smash Dallas in the face.

"Stop! We need him," Thor growled.

Eddie hesitated, then lowered his arm. "Just you wait," he snarled at Dallas. "When this is over, you're dead. You hear me? Dead meat!"

"Damnit!" Thor yelled. "Fucking turn on the juice." Distracted for the moment, he relaxed his grip on Harry.

Harry bit down hard into Thor's arm ... the orderly's screams bounced off the walls. Thor tried to yank away, but Harry hung on, bit down harder.

Eddie had his fingers on the controls when Gina raised her arm up high, pocket knife in her fist. She came down fast and hard, jabbing the blade into his neck.

Eddie's mouth opened but no sound came out; Thor stared, jaw slack, as blood poured from Eddie's neck.

Vinnie removed his restraints, grabbed Thor by the hair, and pulled his head back. Harry chopped hard at his throat.

The orderly dropped like a stone.

Chapter 52

Ziggy sat in the passenger seat of Allison's car, watching the world go by. It was almost as though she could feel the earth rotating, taking an agonizing, painstaking, slow turn. It countered the speed of her frantic mind and she kept asking Allison if she could drive faster.

"We have to get back … have to get to Donnie before those crazy orderlies find him."

"If he's lasted this long taking care of himself, he's probably going to be all right, don't you think?"

"But they'll be coming for the drugs they stole. The ones I told you about."

"How did you find, Donnie … that's the name, right?"

"Yes. That's his name," Ziggy said. "It was pure nosiness on my part. I wanted to look at the place where the female vets had been housed."

"So those vets weren't there when you started working?"

"No. that unit had closed right before Norman became the administrator."

"Why didn't you report Donnie's presence?"

"Oh, I couldn't do that. The poor man was so alone and so easily frightened. He was like a little boy, even with his snow white beard. He was the kind of person that would be swallowed up in a large heartless system like some old shoe."

"Still☐"

"I just couldn't do it." Ziggy turned away from Allison.

"You know, Ziggy" Allison touched her arm "with this whole horrible mess, Bone Point will be vacated and closed almost immediately."

Ziggy nodded. "I know. I've been thinking about that, trying to find a solution for Donnie. He's lost his family and he can't remember much. Maybe with your large database you could help find his mother."

"Maybe," Allison said.

* * *

When Allison and Ziggy drove up to the entrance of Bone Point, there were three sheriff's vehicles, an ambulance, an EMT unit, and an unmarked car parked in front.

"Well, thanks for nothing," Allison said.

"What's the matter?"

"I called an agent in the DEA, told him about the drugs, but asked him to wait until we were done before checking it out. But there's the fool standing in front of his car."

Allison was out of her car and up to the agent in a flash. "Hey, you! I thought we had a deal."

Ziggy couldn't hear the rest. She'd left the car and was running inside the building.

* * *

Gina, Harry, and Vinnie were in the lobby watching one of the sheriffs cuff an orderly.

"Looks liked you're headed back to lockup, Thor." Vinnie grinned. "This time for murder."

Gina joined in. "But don't worry, you won't be lonely. As soon as Eddie's stitched up, he'll join you. That idiot's lucky I barely nicked an artery and was able to compress the wound to save his miserable life." Gina turned to Harry. "What do you think, Harry? Lucky?"

Harry put an arm around her shoulder and kissed her cheek. "He's not lucky. I'm Lucke."

The sheriff read Thor his Miranda rights. "Do you understand?"

Thor was silent.

"I asked you a question, man."

Thor croaked out, "Yes."

Vinnie and Harry slapped out a high five. Harry whispered, "Nothing like a chop to the voice box to shut someone up. No smart-ass remarks out of him for awhile."

Thor whispered, "We've done nothing wrong. You don't have anything on us." But when Thor saw Ziggy, he shut up. For the first time, he really looked scared.

Gina called out, "Ziggy! I was worried about you. Where were you?"

"I was at the Inspector General's office, talking to an agent about what's been going on in this hospital." She looked around. "Where are Norman ... and Delores?"

"Delores left in handcuffs," Gina said. "Norman's missing in action. They've sent in some county people to fill in and take care of the patients until they can be transferred."

"Norman's probably headed for the hills," Harry said. "That's where cowards usually hide."

"I don't think so," Ziggy said. "He was checking out air service. I'll bet he's flown out of the country. That kind always gets away with everything."

The emergency medical techs were wheeling out Dallas, who gave them a thumbs-up.

"How's it going, dude?" Vinnie asked Dallas.

"Just a lot of fuss. But when I get out, this time I'm going home." He handed a piece of paper to Vinnie. "Don't be a stranger. You bring Helen down to visit. That's my folks' home. I'll be staying there for a while."

Vinnie grabbed his hand. "Thanks for everything. I'd have been lost without you."

* * *

Ziggy stepped out of the elevator on the hospital's fifth floor, happy for the first time in months. Donnie was standing by the window watching what was going on down below.

"Hi, Donnie."

When he turned to her, there were tears in his eyes. "I thought you were never coming back."

253

"I wouldn't leave you. Didn't I tell you, we'd find your mother? Now come here and give Ziggy a big hug."

Donnie ran into her open arms and sobbed on her shoulder. "I was so scared."

"You don't have to be scared. I'm taking you home with me and we *will* find your mother. Now let's get your things together."

They went to his hidden spot and she could see that other than the fresh clothes she'd brought, there were only bits of this and that, and piles of spoons and forks, along with several bars of soap in a metal pot.

When she looked more closely at the silverware, she saw something was out of place in the collection. She reached into the bowl and lifted out a set of soldier's dog tags.

Ziggy couldn't quite read what it said.

She took out her phone and turned on the flashlight. The embossed name glinted in the light:

Donaldo Carlos Escondido.

Chapter 53

Sunday, 6:30 pm

Gina, Harry, Vinnie, and Helen sat around the Luckes' kitchen table after a huge spaghetti and meatball dinner.

"Don't you guys ever get tired of S&MBs?" Helen waved a hand, and then pointed to each and everyone around the table.

"Helen Trent, do you and Vinnie ever get tired of hamburgers?" Gina asked.

Helen shot back, "Oh, come on. Everyone knows that's soul food." She closed her eyes and lifted her hands, palms up. "It's like breathing air."

"Hey, as long as you do the cooking … I'll eat anything." Vinnie's face had begun to relax and he was slowly becoming himself again after being home for two weeks.

"Oops, Baby X did it again." Gina broke out into a huge smile.

Harry reached over and rested his hand on her middle. "Wow! Those kicks seem to be getting harder." He bent over and laid his head on her belly. "I just love it."

"What did the doctor say today?" Helen asked.

"Same old thing. Everything is fine. Stay close to your bed or sofa."

"Our fearless Gina didn't tell him about Bone Point and her running around the hospital," Harry said.

"Why give the man a heart attack? He's on the elderly side. Can't take a chance of shocking him to death."

"You better watch her, Harry. As her brother, I can tell you she's never been much good at taking orders."

"I knew that before, but after this last escapade, I'm totally convinced." Harry laughed. "But we all know Gina."

"I can't help it. I have to say it again and again just how grateful I am that she didn't stand on the sidelines." Helen got up, walked around the table, and gave Gina a big kiss and hug. "And Harry, what would Gina have done without you?"

"I have some more news for you two." Vinnie pointed to Gina and Harry. Helen went back to her seat as Vinnie held up what looked like a computer-printed copy of a letter.

Harry and Gina said in unison, "Who's that from?"

Vinnie waved the letter in the air. "It's from Ziggy."

"Oh, how is she?" Gina asked. "She's a real hero."

"Well, she found Donnie's mother and he's now home with his family." Everyone started clapping.

"He's with his mom, his brothers and sisters. They all thought he was dead and they were so happy to have him back. That's what Ziggy says in her letter."

"I hope someone can help him," Harry said.

"What counts is that he's with his family. I know that better than anyone." Vinnie reached for Helen's hand. Soon they had all joined hands around the table and were ginning at each other.

"But there's more here," Vinnie said. "Ziggy has been helping the IG agent go through Bone Point's files. It seems Norman kept a copy of a letter Guy wrote to me before he died. The administrator must have gotten rid of the original, but he'd scanned it and kept it in his files."

"Wow, that's a surprise." Gina's rubbed at her cheeks. "You'd think he would have thrown it away."

"Maybe he felt guilty," Vinnie said. "It seems there were a number of letters that he copied."

"Do you think that maybe there was a *tiny s*park of humanity left in him?" Helen asked.

"No way," Gina said. "Not after the things he did."

Vinnie held the paper up to read, but for a moment he bowed his head as though he couldn't go on.

Helen wrapped an arm around his shoulders. "Do you want me to read it?"

256

"No, no. *I* have to read it." He took a few deep breaths and began:

Dear Vinnie,

   I shouldn't have left without saying goodbye, but I knew I was at the end of the road and I didn't want you to try and stop me.

   Since I returned to civilian life you were the only one who cared about me in any way. Yeah, there was the group, but it never lessened the pain that was ripping my guts out every day. I served my country in the best way I could, but in the end, I didn't seem to matter to anyone but you: the last man from our inner circle.

   I hope you know that I love you, brother.

                                                    Guy

When Vinnie finished reading the letter, they were all crying. Gina went to her brother, so did Harry and Helen.

Soon, they were a mass of hugging bodies.

"Nothing heals like love," Gina whispered.

# # #

About the Authors

Bette Golden Lamb & & J. J. Lamb have co-authored a dozen crime novels, plus a few other individual fiction titles as both books and short stories.

Bette is not only a writer, she's an award-winning painter, sculptor, and ceramist. She's also an RN and knows Gina Mazzio quite well.

J. J. has spent his entire career behind a keyboard as journalist, freelance writer, editor, and fiction

author, plus, when the occasion demands, he's a competent jack-of-all-trades.

The Lambs have lived in Virginia, New Mexico, New York, Nevada, and currently make their home in Northern California. If you see them at a writers' conference, or anyplace else, say *Hello!*